14 Days

MYSTERY OF THE SECRET STOWAWAY

by JOAN LOWERY NIXON
Illustrated by Joan Drescher

Eleven-year-old Joe Riley seems to get into all kinds of trouble since his mother died. The housekeeper who looks after him is constantly complaining to his father.

Fearful that his last escapade will really bring the house down on him, Joe stows away on a cruise ship going to Mexico where his father, a camera technician, is on a film job.

Joe manages to get on board by tagging along with the Handy family. All eight children have red hair and freckles, same as Joe has. Even though his pet hate is girls, Joe is forced into an alliance with bossy Harriet Handy, when she promises to pass him off as one of her brothers.

Poking his nose into everything on the ship, Joe soon realizes that something strange is going on. And Harriet is thrilled to join him in solving the mystery of the man who hates dogs, the strange secretary, and the missing passenger.

This exhuberant story, with its fresh approach, has humor in addition to a lively mystery. It will be thoroughly enjoyed by boys and girls.

MYSTERY OF THE SECRET STOWAWAY

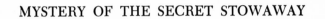

Joan Lowery Nixon

MYSTERY

OF THE

SECRET

STOWAWAY

Illustrated by Joan Drescher

Criterion Books
NEW YORK

by the same author

Mystery of the Grinning Idol
Mystery of Hurricane Castle
Mystery of the Haunted Woods
Mystery of the Hidden Cockatoo

To my son,

Joe

Contents

MYSTERY OF THE SECRET STOWAWAY

1

Nothing But Trouble

I always seem to be in trouble, and it's never my fault. Well, most of the time it isn't. It certainly wasn't my fault when Mrs. Crumbacher got so mad at me.

"Joe Riley!" she kept yelling. "You are the worst eleven-year-old troublemaker I've ever laid eyes on!"

And all I had been trying to do was make someone happy.

Mrs. Crumbacher is the lady I live with when my dad is away on location with a movie crew. He's a technician, which means that he helps to move cameras and furniture and scenery used on movie sets, and all sorts of things like that. It's a real neat job, and he says he meets lots of crazy people and lots of nice people. The only trouble is that he has to go away for months at a time when the company is making movies in another place besides Los Angeles, where we live.

11

That's where Mrs. Crumbacher comes in. Since my mom died two years ago, I have to stay with somebody. I'd much rather go with my dad, but the city of Los Angeles has some dumb rule about kids having to go to school; so it's good-bye Dad, hello Mrs. Crumbacher. Even when school is out for the summer, like right now, I still have to stay with her if Dad isn't back.

I shouldn't complain about her too much because she's not such a bad old lady. She's sort of plump and talks a lot and gets awfully excited about nothing at all; but she's a real good cook. The worst thing about her is the monster who lives with her, Cissy Crumbacher. She's thirteen years old with long dark hair and bangs that hang in her eyelashes. She's silly and stupid and mean all the way through. Dad thinks she's nice, and says boys my age just don't like girls, which shows how wrong even the best grownups can be at times.

It was Cissy's balloon that started the whole problem. It was a big silver balloon filled with helium, which made it float up high at the end of its string.

"Here, little boy," she said, handing it to me when she came home from shopping with one of her girl friends. "I found this in the store and thought it would be nice for a child your age."

I didn't mind getting a balloon. I've always sort of liked balloons, but I wasn't going to let Cissy know that. She and her friend were giggling and snickering. I just took the balloon to my room and tied it to the bedpost.

12

Then I walked back through the living room, where the girls were still acting like a couple of nitwits.

"Funny where a balloon like that is likely to turn up," I said. That would give old Cissy something to think about. I really didn't know yet what I'd do with the balloon, but she didn't know that I didn't know.

Outside I thought I'd get my football and kick it around for awhile, but Mrs. Crumbacher was talking away with the lady next door, Mrs. Goldfinch. They both were yapping a mile a minute, and I wondered if they ever got tired of listening to each other. But I guess they didn't because nearly every day they were out there, Mrs. Crumbacher leaning against the low board fence and Mrs. Goldfinch hanging out of her upstairs apartment window.

It happened they were talking about flying saucers, and it sounded so interesting I sat down on the steps of the back porch to listen. They didn't even know or care that I was there.

"I heard they've got men in them, and they come from Russia," Mrs. Crumbacher said.

Mrs. Goldfinch shook her head so hard it should have rattled. "Not on your life," she said. "Don't you know if Russia had flying saucers we'd have heard about it ages ago?"

"Maybe so," Mrs. Crumbacher said.

"They're from outer space. Take my word for it."

"The air force says they're swamp gas."

"Which shows how much they know," Mrs. Goldfinch said.

"A whole lot of people in Michigan saw one of

14

them," Mrs. Crumbacher's eyes got kind of glittery. "So there's proof."

"People all over Texas have seen them too." Mrs. Goldfinch gave a big sigh that made her shake like a bowl of custard pudding. "People in Texas get to see all kinds of things."

"Maybe because it's so flat."

"Maybe so."

I was still trying to figure that one out when Mrs. Goldfinch got sort of excited and said, "I don't think it's fair that in a big city like Los Angeles nobody has actually seen one up close."

"Would you really want to see one?" Mrs. Crumbacher asked her. "I think I'd be scared."

"Not me," Mrs. Goldfinch said. "I think it would be a thrilling experience. It would be like outer space was contacting me."

I got the funniest picture of a flying saucer floating past with everyone in it waving at Mrs. Goldfinch, and then for no reason at all, I thought of the big silver balloon. And the more I thought about it, the more an interesting idea seemed to grow.

I went into my bedroom where I could think better, because now they had started talking about making turkey soup, which is nothing I need to know about. I sat on the edge of the bed looking at the balloon as it shimmered and wavered in the light breeze from the open window.

I could use my felt marking pen to draw portholes and faces on the balloon and fix some cardboard around the bottom so the balloon end wouldn't show. Then, at night, I could tie some extra

15

string onto the balloon, let it up opposite Mrs. Gold-finch's window, and turn my flashlight on it from below. It's one of those flashlights that can change from red to green to white and would make the balloon look almost like a real saucer.

It was easy to imagine how happy Mrs. Goldfinch would be when she thought she was really seeing a flying saucer, and then how she and Mrs. Crumbacher would have a good laugh together the next day when I showed them the balloon.

That evening, about nine o'clock, it was just beginning to get good and dark. Cissy was on the phone, as usual. If some important geologist was ever going to telephone to warn us that a gigantic earthquake was on the way and we should escape, or if the sheriff was to phone to warn that a dangerous criminal was loose and was heading for our house, we'd just have to die, I guess, because they could never get Cissy off that phone to give us the message.

Mrs. Crumbacher was watching the summer re-runs on television, and it looked like a good chance to show Mrs. Goldfinch the saucer. I took the balloon and went through the kitchen, out the back door, and onto the driveway below the window of Mr. and Mrs. Goldfinch's apartment.

I saw in a movie once that someone outside who wanted to signal someone in the house threw some light rocks against the window. I looked around the flower beds in the dark, nearly breaking my toe on the water pipe, and finally found a handful of little cement chips from the edge of the driveway.

They must not make windows as strong as they

16

used to because those little chips went right through the window pane, making a real smashing sound of broken glass. I barely had time to get the balloon in position before Mrs. Goldfinch pushed up the window with a bang, looked out, and yelled, "Who did that?"

I turned the flashlight on the balloon, switching from red to green and back to red. She looked at the balloon, and her mouth dropped wide open. Her eyes got bigger and bigger until they were practically popping out of her head. Then she screamed so loud my eardrums hurt, turned around, and fainted with a terrible slamming noise on her living room floor.

Mr. Goldfinch stuck his head way out the window, took a look at the balloon, and another meaner look at me, and said he was going to see I got sent to prison.

By this time Mrs. Crumbacher and Cissy were outside too, and Mrs. Crumbacher quieted him down, and I said I'd pay for the broken window pane out of some of the money my dad left with me, and Mrs. Goldfinch got up and started getting mad at everybody, even her husband. So Mrs. Crumbacher marched me inside and sent me to my bedroom and said I couldn't have desserts for two weeks. This made me feel bad because I knew for a fact she was going to make German chocolate cake the next day, and besides I really hadn't done anything.

I lay on my bed and looked at a comic book, but I kept thinking about how long it had been since I'd seen my dad and remembering how it used to be when I'd hug my mother. I felt like hugging somebody right then, but I didn't have anybody. If I couldn't

17

have my mother or my dad, I wished I could have a dog; but Mrs. Crumbacher was allergic to dogs. A dog would really be nice to hold when everybody was mad. He wouldn't blame me for things. He'd just be glad I was there.

I squished the pillow up in a ball and wrapped my arms around it, which was better than nothing; and I went to sleep with my clothes on, which I knew Mrs. Crumbacher didn't like. She said it was unsanitary.

Tomorrow, I thought, tomorrow I'm going to take some of the money Dad left with me and go for a long bus ride. I didn't even care where I was going just as long as I could transfer twice. At least I couldn't get into any trouble riding around on a bus.

2

Trapped!

It was all right with Mrs. Crumbacher if I wanted to ride a bus. I think she was glad to get me out of the house. On Tuesday mornings she likes to iron and watch television, and it seems to make her nervous when I slam the handball against the side of the house or fight with Cissy.

I walked down to the corner and got the express bus that goes downtown. When I got to the terminal I'd see where I wanted to go from there. I like to ride busses because the seats are up higher than they are in cars and there's always so much to look at.

We turned onto the Hollywood freeway, heading downtown. At that time of the day there wasn't too much traffic, so we really zipped along. We went past the big hospital where I was born, and I had to smile as I remembered how my dad said he'd have known me anywhere, without anybody even telling him which was his baby, because I had red hair and freckles. Mom would giggle and tell him that babies didn't have freckles, but he said they were right underneath, ready to come out, and he could see them even if no one else could.

The bus sped past Echo Park. Sometimes I like to go to Echo Park and feed the ducks—not in the summer when all the tourists are feeding them and they're stuffed, but in the winter when they get real hungry and nearly go crazy at the sight of dried bread crumbs.

After awhile we went off the freeway and down one of the avenues. It was slower now, with the bus having to stop at stop signs and red lights. There were a lot more people, too, who were shopping or working downtown. Finally we crossed Main Street, which is really a crummy-looking street, and pulled into the terminal.

I still hadn't thought much about where I wanted to go next, but there was a big bus, almost ready to pull out, with a sign saying, "Wilmington, Harbor Area."

That sounded good to me. I might get to see some ships, and I hadn't been to Wilmington or the harbor before. I bought a ticket and climbed aboard. We went back to the harbor freeway and headed south, and there were a lot of good things to look at, like used car lots and hamburger stands and stuff like that.

It didn't take long before the bus was off the freeway and making stops in traffic again. Most of the people got off, and finally the driver pulled up to a corner and turned around to look at me.

"This is as far as we go," he said.

I got up and walked to the front of the bus. "Where do I go to see the ships?"

He pointed ahead of us. "You gotta keep walking that way for a few blocks."

"Thanks, sir," I said. My father taught me to say, "sir," so once in awhile I remember to say it.

"That's all right, kid," the driver said, and he smiled at me. "Say, if you want to see one of those fancy ocean liners, just turn right when you get down to the docks. There's a big one getting ready to take off for Mexico and South America—real pretty ship. They let visitors aboard to say good-bye to the passengers. You might have a chance to look it over."

"That sounds good," I told him. "Thanks a lot." I forgot to put on the "sir," but he didn't seem to notice. I jumped down from the bus. "See you around!" I called. He waved back at me, and I set off in the direction he had pointed out.

I could smell the salty tang of the ocean, and I almost ran, I was so eager to get there. I turned right, as the bus driver had told me, and went into some big barny sheds full of people. They were all dressed up as though they were going to a party; I was glad I had changed my jeans before I took the bus ride. My slacks were my good ones without any holes in the knees because I usually wear them to church where I don't do much fighting; and my shirt was a nice one my dad had sent me from Mexico last Easter. So all in all, I didn't feel out of place.

I was just standing there looking at all the people rushing around and yelling at each other and some of them hugging and kissing, when I noticed a guy in a uniform giving me a funny look.

He took a few steps over to me and said, "Hey, kid, who are you with?"

"Why should I have to be with somebody?" I asked him.

"Don't be smart aleck with me," he said. He took off his hat and scratched his head where the hair was plastered down with sweat. "Every kid has got to be with somebody or they don't belong here."

Well, golly, I hadn't even seen the ocean, let alone the big ship, and it seemed like a dumb rule to me, so I just took a quick look around, and what do you know! Nearby was a family with about a million little kids in it, and all of them had red hair and freckles.

The guard took a step closer to me and reached out to grab my shoulder, but I gave a quick sidestep and squeezed up my face like I was going to cry.

"Mama!" I whined, "that man's gonna hit me!"

Quick like anything I made a dash for the family with the red hair and got right in the middle of them. The guard frowned at me and walked back to the entrance to the shed.

That was really a nutty family. I counted the kids, and there were eight of them, a couple of them almost as big as me, but they were all yelling at once and running around each other at the same time. They reminded me of a lot of baby chicks. Their mother and father were standing together, talking calmly, as though they didn't even have any children. The mother hen of the crowd was a tall teen-ager who kept grabbing out at the kids as they ran around her and saying over and over, "I think I'm going out of my mind!"

The crowd began to move toward the opposite end of the shed, and I went right along. I figured the ship had to be where we were going. The mother and father walked on ahead, and an old lady near us, who was all wrapped up in a huge fur coat, stuck her head out of the collar like a turtle and asked the teen-aged girl, "Are you the big sister of this remarkable family?"

The girl looked kind of pitiful for a moment and said, "No, I just answered their ad in the newspaper. They hired me to baby-sit for the cruise, so the mother could relax."

"How lovely for you," the old lady said.

The girl gave another grab, as one little boy chased another right under her nose, almost knocking her down. "I think I'm going out of my mind," she said.

All of a sudden I felt a pull on my hand, and when I looked down I saw this little girl no higher than my hips. She was grinning up at me and must have thought I was a relative. I grinned back.

"Pick me up," she demanded.

"Why not?" I didn't mind carrying her, as long as we were both going in the same direction.

In a minute a blast of fresh sea air hit us, and I looked up to see that we had left the shed and were out on the docks with the big white ship in front of us. It was so huge and beautiful I could hardly breathe for a few seconds. More than anything else I wanted to see what it looked like, to get up on the top deck and stare out at the ocean. Just for a few minutes,

23

before the visitors had to get off, I could pretend I was going to sail away and visit my father.

We stepped onto the gangplank, following the mob of people. Nobody in the family I was with had noticed me, except for the little thing I was carrying, which was all right with me.

The biggest girl in the family tugged on the arm of the boy next to her. They were just about the same size and looked a lot alike, except that she was fatter than he was.

"Look down there at the water, Frank," she said. "Look at the way the ship moves back and forth and back and forth. When we get on the ocean, then it's really going to go back and forth and back and forth and back . . ."

Frank punched her on her arm. "Cut it out, Harriet!" he said.

"You know how you always get seasick," she said. "Even in a rowboat, and even when we took a sight-seeing trip up the river! A piddly little river, and you got seasick!"

"Do you want to get thrown overboard?" Frank yelled, hitting her again.

"Don't fight!" The teen-ager grabbed Frank by the shoulder and separated them. "Do you want to drive me out of my mind?"

Just ahead of us a man with a bushy brown beard and a shaggy brown suit almost the same shade was arguing with a guy dressed in what looked like a naval uniform who had a clip board and some papers and was checking the passengers.

"And I tell you that my secretary is aboard because

I sent her on ahead with some things for me," the man said.

"I'm sorry for the confusion, Mr. Riggle," the officer said. "I just didn't have a check by Miss Stanhope's name. Are you sure she actually came aboard?"

Mr. Riggle was getting angry. "Miss Stanhope waved at me!" he said. "She's up on the next deck!"

"I'm sorry, sir. I can't imagine how she came aboard without being checked."

"You made a mistake, young man! That's how it was done!"

"If you wait, Mr. Riggle, I'll have the purser get Miss Stanhope, and we'll check her off the list right now."

Mr. Riggle shook his head. "Check her off anyway. Don't waste her time by bringing her back here. I've got work for her to do!" He stomped off, complaining loudly about inefficiency, and it was our turn.

I was glad I was holding the little kid because I could hide my face behind her, and since the other kids kept shouting and fooling around and chasing in and out, I was sure that no one could count noses.

"The Handy family," the officer said, checking names off the list.

"And Betty Frances," Mrs. Handy said. "She's our little helper on this trip, so I don't have to lift a finger and can relax."

Betty Frances mumbled something under her breath, but the officer gave her the kind of smile you see in toothpaste ads. Her cheeks got red, and she smiled back, and we all stepped aboard the ship.

I put the little girl down on her feet. "Bye-bye," I said. "Go to Mama or you'll get lost."

She ran off with her family, and I hurried in the other direction.

I didn't know whether to go upstairs or downstairs, but the elevator in the hallway was going downstairs, so I did too. The hallways were narrow, and there were a lot of people in them. Before I knew it, I got pushed into a room with a bunch of people all crowded together eating cake and drinking something in paper cups.

A man was filling cups at one side of the stateroom, so I went over and said, "I'd like some, please."

"Oh, no you wouldn't," he said. "It will be plain ginger ale for you.

He poured me a paper cup of ginger ale and handed me a piece of cake on a paper plate. I sat in the corner behind a real fat man and ate it up in a, flash. I hadn't realized I was so hungry. I looked at my watch and saw that it was almost noon, and I hadn't eaten for three hours. I felt kind of weak just thinking about it.

After I finished I worked my way back into the hallway and through some more people until I saw another party going on in another stateroom. This one was even better. They had all kinds of potato chips and stuff to dip them in and some crackers and cheese. I ate a lot until some lady asked me whose little boy I was. I recognized that tone of voice as meaning she thought I was getting more than she was, so I beat it out of there and found another party.

Every once in awhile I passed the same uniformed guy in the hall, and pretty soon he began to give me some funny looks. After the last party I went out into the hall again, and this time there weren't many people. He was down at the end of the hall, and he started toward me. I remembered I hadn't even got on top to look at the ocean, and I didn't want to get thrown off the ship now, so I just stepped into the nearest stateroom and shut the door. Luckily no one was in there, or I would have had to get out in a hurry, but just to play it safe, in case the officer searched the rooms, I scooted under the bed.

I was glad I was there, because in a few minutes the door opened, and a couple of people came in. They closed the door behind them.

"Tonight you're gonna kill 'em," a man said.

There was a long pause, and then a girl answered, "Oh, Jerry!"

"Don't be nervous," he said. "I taught you how to do it. Now, tonight, just go out there and kill 'em. Don't even think about it. Just do it."

I felt the way I did when I fell in the deep end of the Hollywood swimming pool before I learned how to swim. There was a cold feeling crawling along my backbone, and even the ends of my fingers felt numb. I tried not to breathe, so they wouldn't hear me, but I needn't have bothered. I couldn't breathe anyway.

Here were some people planning a murder, and here I was under the bed listening to them. If they knew I was there they'd murder me too.

A deep whistle blew that seemed to shake the whole ship. I could feel it vibrate all through my body. Out in the hallway people were yelling good-bye to one another, and some guy kept shouting, "All ashore who's going ashore!"

I wondered if I'd have a chance if I dashed out to the hallway. If these people in the room had the door locked, I'd be caught. And then . . . I didn't want to be murdered!

The sound of the voices in the hallway drifted off, and soon it was silent. The only sound I could hear was my heart banging and bumping away inside my chest.

The girl began to hum to herself, and I could hear a silky, swishing noise. It sounded like the noise Cissy makes brushing her hair. Gosh! I thought. She's getting ready to murder some poor guy, and she can sit there and hum and brush her hair like any other day in the week.

At first I thought I was shivering, but I realized it was the movement of the ship. The big motors began turning over, and the ship was underway.

I put my head down on my arms and thought what a mess I was in. I was not only going to get murdered if these people found me here, but I was also a stowaway! I tried to think of the words to the prayers I knew as well as I knew my own name, but all that I could think of to say to God was one word—*Help!*

3

Joe Becomes a Stowaway

I heard the door open, and the guy named Jerry said, "I'll see you in awhile, Dodi. I've got to unpack. If you need me, I'll be in my stateroom at the end of the corridor."

"All right," she said, and went on humming.

I began to feel a little better. With only one of them still in the room, and that one only a girl, I had a better chance of escaping. If I could sneak out from under the bed, I could get to the door inside of three seconds flat. I listened carefully when Jerry left, and I knew it wasn't locked. I was practically home safe.

Just then Dodi came over to the bed and flopped down. Unfortunately the bed was low, and the mattress smacked me right where I sit down. Without thinking, I gave an oof-ing sound.

I put my hand over my mouth fast, but I was too late. Overhead I heard Dodi make the kind of squeeking sound girls make when they get all excited about something. I just lay there, trying to think of what to do, but before I could move, a corner of the bedspread was pulled up, and a face was looking at me upside down.

"Good heavens," she said. "For a minute I thought there was somebody under my bed."

"I am somebody," I said.

"I mean a real somebody, like a burglar. You're just a little boy."

"I'm not so little," I said. "I'm eleven."

"Pardon me," she said, and she gave me a big smile. Only upside down the smile looked kind of funny.

"Aren't you going to ask me what I'm doing under your bed?"

"Why should I?" she answered. "You'd only give me some wild story. When I was eleven I was always doing something stupid, so I guess that's all you're doing—something stupid."

"You're right," I said. She wasn't bad for a lady. I began to like her, until I remembered that she was planning to murder someone.

"The blood is rushing to my head," she said. "Why don't you get out of there? It will be easier to talk."

"Are you going to shoot me?"

"No," she said. "Of course not."

You know, even upside down like that she had an honest face, so I believed her and wriggled out from under the bed.

She motioned to a nearby chair. "Sit down," she said.

31

I took a good look at her. She had long blonde hair and a face with a lot of make-up on it, and even with all the make-up she didn't look bad. She reminded me of the girl on the poster in Mr. Adolph's delicatessen.

"You're staring at me," she said. "Do you think I'm pretty?"

I thought that was a silly question. She didn't have any bumps or lumps or anything like that on her face.

"You don't look like a killer," I told her.

"Thank you—I think," she said and looked in the mirror. She started brushing her hair again.

I wanted to get down to business.

"Look," I said, "there's no use sitting around and talking. I heard that Jerry guy tell you to kill somebody, so I know you're planning a murder. I can get to the door before you can, because I'm closer; and I'll tell the captain. I just want to know why a nice lady like you would want to murder someone."

She started to laugh and laugh and almost fell off the bed. I began to wonder if she was some kind of maniac.

Finally she wiped her eyes on the edge of the bedspread and said, "You heard him tell me to 'kill 'em.' That was a show business term. I'm the singer in the ship's nightclub, and this is my first big assignment. Jerry is my agent, and he knows I'm nervous, so he was telling me to 'kill 'em.' He could have said, 'Go out and knock 'em dead.' Don't you know anything about show business?"

"Not much," I admitted. "I've been on studio sets

32

with my dad a couple of times, but he doesn't like me to go there too often."

She clapped her hands together and jumped up. "Oh, you're a movie star's little boy!"

"Well, not exactly," I started to say, but she took my chin in her hands and began studying my face.

"What's your last name?"

"I'd rather not say."

"I can understand that. Lots of important people like to travel incognito." She nodded and smiled. "Isn't it a coincidence, your being here? Because I'm going to be a movie star too!"

"You are? I thought you were a singer."

She walked over to the mirror and took another look. She seemed sort of happy about what she saw there. "I'm a singer now, but I'm going to be a movie star when I learn how to act. Jerry says so."

I started edging toward the door. "I'd better go now," I said.

"Wait a minute," she said. "We haven't told each other our first names. I'm Dodi Doll."

"I'm Joe."

"Is your father here, Joe?" she asked.

"No," I said, hoping she wouldn't guess I didn't belong on the ship. "I'm with some other people."

"Well, have a nice time, Joe," she said. "I'll be seeing you."

I hurried to the elevator and went up to the top deck of the ship to look around. Sure enough, we were quite a way out to sea, and the land looked awfully small behind the ship. I thought how mad Mrs.

33

Crumbacher would be if I had to stop the ship to get put ashore, and I didn't think the captain would be any too happy either. I decided it would be a lot easier just to stay aboard and get off in Mexico and find my dad. He'd sure be surprised when he found out how I got to Mexico, but he'd be glad to see me.

All I had to figure out was what to eat and where to sleep. It shouldn't take more than a few days to get to Mexico. I had almost five dollars, and there was a little shop on the ship that sold candy. I decided I could live on candy for a few days and get my vitamins later. As far as the sleeping was concerned, I'd have to scout around the ship and find a good place.

I took the elevator down to what they called the promenade deck and saw some guy walking around with a big cart. There were all sorts of things on it: little sandwiches that some woman must have dreamed up, because they weren't more than one bite in size, and I thought I'd have to swallow half a plate full of them to feel like I'd had anything to eat; and lots of little cakes and a big pot of something that was probably coffee.

The guy with the cart kept stopping and giving people some of the food. I caught up to him in a hurry. He handed me a plate, and I piled on a lot of the sandwiches and cakes until I noticed him frowning at me.

"I didn't have any lunch," I said, trying to look pitiful.

"I imagine you'll make up for it at dinnertime," he

said. "Just leave some of the afternoon tea for the rest of the passengers."

I walked away from him, munching. I liked a ship that remembered afternoon snacks, especially since I didn't have to spend any of my money. It would make the candy bars stretch out farther.

Up ahead some people were watching something going on at the ship's rail. I put down the empty plate and went over to watch too. Maybe somebody was falling overboard.

I poked my head between two men and saw that it was Dodi Doll. She wasn't falling overboard, but the way she was balancing on the railing with her legs crossed, she could have real easy if someone had given her a push. She was holding a crazy-looking little dog with blue hair that curled all around its ears. I knew it was a miniature poodle, but it was the first time I had ever seen a blue poodle.

The little dog kept yapping and squirming while Dodi tried to hang on to it and not fall off the railing at the same time.

"Jerry," she said, "I told you this dog doesn't like me."

"Make it like you long enough for me to get this picture," a guy with a camera said, and I realized that was her agent, Jerry. "I have to get this picture of you off to the newspapers."

"It's going to bite me," Dodi complained.

I don't know much about dogs since I never had a dog. I only know that I like them, and I could see that the crazy-looking poodle was just scared. I

elbowed my way forward and stepped up to Dodi Doll, taking the dog out of her hands.

I held it in the crook of my arm, stroking its head. The poor little thing was trembling, but it looked up at me and decided to trust me, I guess, because pretty soon it had calmed down and was licking my arm.

"You're wonderful, Joe!" Dodi said. "How did you do it?"

"I don't know," I said. I really didn't.

"Who is this kid?" Jerry asked.

"Joe's a friend of mine." Dodi winked at me.

"Well, Joe," Jerry said, "do you think that you could get that stupid dog to pose for a picture with Dodi?"

The dog gave a little shiver, and I said, "Don't call him stupid. You upset him."

"It's a girl dog," Dodi said. "Her name is Fifi, and she's dyed blue, because that's supposed to be my favorite color, and this is what Jerry calls a publicity stunt, which all girls who are hoping to be movie stars have to do."

"Sounds wild," I said, feeling sorry for the poor dog. I snuggled her closer, and she licked me again.

"It is," Dodi said. "In the first place, I don't like dogs, and, in the second place, blue isn't my favorite color. Lavender is, but some other movie star already chose lavender."

"Give her the dog, kid," Jerry said. "We're wasting time."

I started to hand the dog to Dodi, but poor Fifi began to tremble. I held her close again and said, "Look, Feef." I just couldn't call a dog a dumb name like Fifi. "Feef, old girl, this is something like going to school or to the dentist. You just gotta get it done and over with. Just let the lady hold you long enough to take the pictures, and then you'll be through. Get the message?"

I don't believe in dogs understanding English, but I know that old Feef could tell I was explaining something to her straight. She let me hand her to Dodi.

I stepped out of the way, and the pictures were taken. Jerry went off with his big camera, and Dodi hopped off the rail. Feef wiggled and yipped and could hardly wait to get back to me.

Dodi sighed. "I know it's silly to offer money to the son of a famous movie star," she said, "but would it be all right if I hired you to take care of Fifi on this trip? She doesn't like me, and I don't like her."

"Sure," I said, "I'll take care of her, and I don't mind getting paid one little bit."

"She stays in the ship's kennels most of the time," Dodi said. "But I feel sorry for her down there, even if I don't like her much. She ought to get some exercise."

Feef licked my chin. "I'll be glad to exercise her," I said. Maybe I could even sleep with her. I'd have to see what the layout was like in the kennels.

Dodi Doll gave me Feef's leash and told me she'd see me later. Feef and I took off around the ship. I was a little worried that walking along with a blue poodle would make me look conspicuous, but everyone stared at the dog instead of at me.

It was fun to go around the promenade. Feef was really perking along, and I was walking faster and faster. I guess we went around a corner too quickly, because Feef and I ran right into that guy with the beard—Mr. Riggle.

He glared at me, and before I knew what he was up to, he hauled off and kicked Feef out of the way. She yipped and whimpered and ran behind me to hide.

"Hey!" I yelled. "You kicked my dog!"

"I did not," he said. "I merely moved it out of the way."

"But you hurt her!"

He didn't even answer. He just nudged past me, pushing me against the wall. I picked up Feef, and we watched Mr. Riggle charging down the promenade. He was about the meanest man I'd ever run into. I had the creepy feeling that I was going to meet up with him again and that the next time there was going to be real trouble.

4

A Conspirator

I held Feef and told her that I wasn't going to let old Mr. Riggle even get near her again and she should just trust me to take good care of her. I had to hold her close, because she was trembling all over. She sure did tremble a lot, but I guess if someone dyed me blue and took my picture and then I got kicked by a character with a wild-looking beard, I'd be a little bit shaky too.

The sun was going down over the ocean, and I just had to sit there and look for awhile. It was as pretty as a technicolor movie, with the water all speckly golden and the sky on fire right down to the horizon. Feef and I were very quiet, just watching, for a long time, and then her stomach rumbled. Or maybe it was mine. Or both of us. Anyhow, I guess we were hungry, and I had to see about feeding her before I could feed myself.

I asked a big guy in a uniform where the kennels were and took Feef down to them on the elevator. They were on the very bottom deck, which the guy said was the main deck. It was on the same deck as the dining room, and I could smell the dinner being cooked. I could hardly stand it, I got so hungry.

The kennels were all right, I guess, and the attendant locked Feef into a roomy enough cage and gave her something to eat. She was a nice little dog. Even though she was hungry, she took time to look at me and wag her tail before she started to eat. Most of my friends aren't that polite. The only trouble was that there was no place in those kennels where I could sleep without getting caught. I'd have to find another place.

Well, Feef was settled, and I had to start thinking about my own dinner. That food smelled better and better, and the idea of just eating candy bars was kind of sickening. I went down the corridor to the dining room entrance and watched a few people going in. I didn't want to tangle with any of those uniformed guys, so I went up to an old lady who seemed to be waiting for somebody and asked her how much the dinners cost.

"Oh, dear boy," she said. "They don't cost anything. The meals are included with the price of your ticket. Your parents should have told you that."

"I forgot to ask anyone," I said. "Do we just go in and sit down and eat?"

"You have a seat and table assigned to you," she said. "For goodness sakes, go find your parents and

41

don't be so impatient. They'll explain everything to you."

I remembered to say "thank you" and slowly walked away down the corridor. I guess that let me out for good. My stomach was making a fearful noise by this time, and I wished there was some way for my brain to tell it that it would just have to shut up and wait its turn.

The elevator door opened, and that crazy Handy family swarmed out all around me. At least the children and the girl named Betty Frances did. The parents must have decided to eat later in peace and quiet. Betty Frances was trying to count noses and kept saying, "Is everyone here? Is everyone here?"

The kids all had funny looks on their faces, as though they knew something she didn't, especially that Harriet. Then one of the little boys pulled at Harriet's sleeve and said in a loud whisper, "We aren't going to tell her that Frank is seasick, are we?"

"Keep quiet," Harriet whispered. "You'll spoil everything."

Another boy who looked just like the first one and must have been his twin said, "You told us you were going to play a trick on Betty Frances! What is it?"

"If I told you everything, you'd just tell," Harriet said. "Now, be quiet."

It wasn't hard to figure out that poor Betty Frances was going to get everybody seated and then find an empty chair and have to try to figure out what to do. Harriet was undoubtedly going to pull something with that empty chair, but she hadn't told the other kids what.

42

An empty chair! The thought suddenly hit me. It was obvious that this Betty Frances didn't know the kids very well yet. Maybe she wouldn't realize I wasn't Frank. I was about the same size as Frank, with the same coloring as all of them, and maybe the other kids wouldn't give me away if I told them I was starving to death. The littlest girl put her hand into mine and said, "Hi." That made up my mind. I'd give it a try. It was better than eating candy bars.

I marched into the dining room right along with them, and nobody looked at me twice. The kids piled into chairs around a big round table, with a few people smiling and saying, "Isn't that cute?" A few people who were sitting at tables close to us looked nervous. I sat down next to Harriet, and all the littlest ones sat on the other side, next to Betty Frances.

Finally Betty Frances looked around the table, gave a sigh of relief, and said, "Well, everyone's here. Thank goodness!"

All of the kids looked at each other; then they all looked at me. Everyone thought I was part of Harriet's trick on Betty Frances, so not one of them let on, except one dumb kid who said, "Hi, Frank," and laughed so hard he knocked over his water glass.

In all the confusion of mopping the water up, Harriet turned to me and said in a low voice, "OK, Buster. Who are you, and what are you doing here?"

"They ran out of room at my table and sent me over here."

"Ha!" she said.

"Well," I tried again. "I'm tired of sitting with my

44

parents. My dad is real mean and makes me eat my vegetables. I'd rather sit here with your family."

Her eyes glittered. "Ha, ha!" she said.

There was no fooling this Harriet. She was a real cool character. So I told her the truth about getting on board just to see what the boat looked like, and staying on board by mistake when the boat left, and how I was now going to go as far as Mexico to be with my father, who was working there with a movie crew. When I finished she just glared at me.

"You expect me to believe some crazy story like that?"

I gave a big sigh. "No," I said. "I expect you to tell somebody I don't belong on the ship, and they'll throw me in jail."

She gave a sneaky smile and said, "I wouldn't do that. I just want you to tell me the truth."

I never met such a dumb girl. Most of the girls I know are dumb, but this one was the dumbest. The trouble with girls is they get an idea in their heads and nobody can get it out. I didn't know what to say to Harriet, because I didn't know who she thought I was supposed to be. I decided to let her tell me.

I leaned close to her and pretended to be mysterious. "Suppose you tell me what you've guessed, and I'll tell you if you're right or not."

Harriet liked this idea. She gave a little bounce in her chair and said, "I'm pretty smart. I know a lot about you."

I knew something about Harriet too. I knew why Frank liked to hit her.

"First of all," Harriet said, "you ran away from home."

She looked at me searchingly, and I just said, "Go on."

"Well," she said, acting even more confident, "either you did something terrible, or somebody did something terrible to you. Which was it?"

"Somebody did something terrible to me," I said quickly. I didn't want her to think I was a criminal or anything like that.

She thought for a moment. "Somebody beat you and didn't feed you—a stepmother, I bet."

I thought about Mrs. Crumbacher saying I couldn't have desserts for two weeks. "Go on," I said.

Harriet was really getting warmed up now. "And when you ran away they didn't dare tell the police, so they sent someone after you to bring you back. You escaped, but he trailed you to this ship, and he's probably on it right now!"

I could see what Harriet did in her spare time. She watched too much television, that's what.

Harriet sighed and leaned close to me, her face just a couple of inches from mine. She smelled of some kind of stinky perfume and some jam that was smudged on her cheek. It nearly made me sick being that close to a girl.

"We'll never give you away—never! You can be Frank Handy as long as you want and eat all his meals, because he's going to keep on being seasick. I promise."

The waiter came and put down big bowls of steaming tomato soup. Nothing had ever looked so good to me in my life. I thought about all those lovely meals going to waste because Frank couldn't eat them and about this crazy girl who only believed what she wanted to believe, no matter what I said. It was very tempting.

"What's your name?" Harriet said.

"Joe," I said. "Just Joe."

She nodded. "People who are escaping never give their last names. Don't worry. I won't insist."

The waiters kept bringing more and more food, and I really ate a lot. Every once in awhile one of the other children would look at me and giggle, but each time I just winked back, and that seemed to make them happy enough.

When we got to the dessert I hardly had any room left, which was a new experience for me. I looked up and saw Mr. Riggle come into the dining room and follow a waiter to a table nearby. The waiter said something to him, and Mr. Riggle said loudly, "Miss Stanhope isn't feeling too well. She decided to skip dinner."

Harriet nudged me. "You've been staring at that man with the beard. He looks mean."

"He is mean," I said.

Harriet gave a satisfied nod. "Maybe he's the one they sent after you."

"I don't think so," I said. Even though I didn't like Mr. Riggle, I hated to think of what might happen to him if Harriet decided to help me escape from him.

"Don't be silly. Of course he is," Harriet said. "Look at his awful beard. That proves it."

I just shrugged. It didn't do any good to tell Harriet

47

anything. She lit into a piece of lemon cream pie as though she had never had anything to eat, but I just sat there and thought things out. It looked as though I had most of my meals taken care of as long as Frank stayed seasick, but I still had one problem to take care of. Where was I going to sleep?

5

A Mysterious Bundle

Harriet had the sleeping problem worked out too. When we finished dinner she said, "Come back to our staterooms with us. We don't want Betty Frances to get suspicious, and she will if you just walk off."

I didn't mind, especially since the littlest Handy kid made me carry her again. Being carried around was a real thing with her, and I wondered if all little kids were like that, or if she just liked being up in the air, or if her feet hurt. It wasn't any use to ask her. She just said, "Hi" and "Pick me up," and hardly anything more than that.

When we got to the staterooms the Handys were staying in, I could see they were on the upper deck— the same as Dodi Doll's stateroom, but on the opposite side of the ship. In between was a closed-off place with a few doors on it. One was marked "Gymnasium," and another "Washer and Dryer." The last one gave me a good idea—a way I could get clean clothes. Only what would happen if someone came in while I was washing and drying everything I had on? I would have to give that problem some more thought.

Betty Frances took the little girl out of my arms. "Thank you, uh . . . uh . . ."

"Frank," Harriet said.

"I'll put Amy to bed," Betty Frances said, and she went into the stateroom next door.

"All of us girls sleep in there with Betty Frances," Harriet said, "and the boys sleep in this stateroom. The one next to the girls' is our parents' room."

She gathered the other kids around her in a huddle and said, "This is Joe. Joe is running away from some cruel people, and we are going to save him."

"I don't need you to save me," I said, but she just ignored me.

"So most of the time we're going to pretend he's Frank." She lined everyone up and introduced me, although I was just as confused as Betty Frances and couldn't remember all the names at first. It seemed that Harriet and Frank were twins and were ten years old. Laura was nine, Joanne was eight, Peter was seven, Bill and John were another set of twins, five years old, and Amy was two. They were all kind of wild, but Harriet was the boss of the crew, and they paid attention to her.

"Bill and John can sleep together, and Joe can have Bill's bunk," Harriet said.

"Hey! I don't want to take anyone's bed."

"They like to sleep together," Harriet said. "At home they do. Don't you, boys?"

"Only when it's cold," Bill said.

"Bill kicks in his sleep," John said.

Harriet opened the stateroom door, and we all followed her inside. Mostly I wanted to see Frank, since I was supposed to be Frank.

Frank lay in bed, looking at a magazine.

"Who's that?" he asked, staring at me. He wasn't a very friendly guy.

"This is Joe," Harriet told him.

"Hi," I said.

Peter said, "Some people are after him to put him in jail, so we're going to let him sleep in here."

"Yeah?" Frank began to look interested.

"One of those ugly stepmother cases," Harriet said.

"Big deal," Frank said, and looked bored again.

"How do you feel?" Harriet asked him.

"A little better," Frank said. "Maybe I can eat with you tomorrow."

Harriet took a quick look at me and turned back to Frank. "I'm surprised that you feel better in this weather," she said, "especially with the ship going up and down, back and forth . . ." She made big sweeping motions with her hands.

Frank's face puckered up, and he slid down under the covers.

"And all that food you missed tonight, Frank. There was gravy, kind of greasy, watery-looking gravy, and funny looking oysters, which were kind of squishy and wiggly and . . ."

51

"Cut it out, Harriet!" Frank sounded half choked under the blankets. "Go away and leave me alone."

Harriet walked me to the door. "It's all in his mind," she said. "Believe me, it will last the whole trip."

I could see why, and I felt sorrier than ever for Frank, and just a little bit guilty for eating his dinner.

"He could starve to death," I said.

"Oh, no. I keep bringing him things like bouillon soup and stuff that's easy to swallow."

She opened the door and stuck her head out, looking both ways. "Betty Frances will come back to check on us in a few minutes and send us into our staterooms to get ready for bed." She frowned as she thought. "Mother and Daddy said they'd come by to check us too, about ten o'clock. Do you think you could stay away until then?"

"Sure," I said.

"If you come back a little after ten, the boys will let you in."

I nodded and stepped into the corridor, and Harriet shut the door behind me. Just in case Betty Frances came out the other door, I left in a hurry.

I had a couple of hours to kill, so I decided to see Feef before she went to sleep. I took the stairway down to the main deck and went into the kennels.

The guy in charge of the kennels smiled at me in a friendly way. "How come your dog is blue, kid?"

"She's not my dog," I told him. "I just promised the lady who owns her that I'd watch out for her on the cruise."

Feef had run over to the side of her cage, and as I bent down to pet her she licked my fingers like crazy and wagged her funny tail and whined as though she was trying to talk to me.

"Did the lady tell you why the dog is blue?"

"She said it was a publicity stunt." I scratched in back of Feef's ears. "Do you think that blue will wear off?"

"Oh, sure," the guy said. "The dog's hair will grow fast in winter, and the blue color will grow out in no time."

I played with Feef for awhile, but I could see that the guy wanted to close up for the night. I told Feef I'd be back for her in the morning.

"That dog sure seems to like you a lot," he said as I got up.

I don't know why, but what he said made me feel awfully good, and I whistled all the way to the elevator.

I decided to explore the ship, since it still was a long time to ten o'clock. I went all the way to the top, to the sun deck, but at night, with the breeze from the ocean, it was cold. The ocean was like a pool of black ink all around us, and the way it rose and humped under the lights from the ship, I could see how sailors once imagined they saw sea monsters.

At the end of the deck was an observation room, all glassed in, but it was full of grownups and was the wrong place for me to be.

I went down a deck, but there were only offices and the wheel house and a few cabins, which probably belonged to the ship's crew. So I caught the elevator again and went down to the boat deck. This was the deck where the lifeboats were hung, and I thought how I could have slept in a lifeboat, if I had only thought of it.

I climbed up on one of the lifeboat supports and tried to shinny up to take a look under the canvas that was laced across it, but some officer yelled, "Hey, kid, get down from there!" I scrambled back down and hurried out of his way. This ship sure was full of a lot of official people.

At the back end of the ship—the stern, I guess it's called—there was a balcony overlooking the promenade deck. From this balcony anybody could watch the people down there in the swimming pool, although right now there wasn't anyone in the pool. I guess it was too cold.

I walked down to the promenade deck and took a turn around the swimming pool, but it was lonely and dark. I went up to the center, where I could peek in the windows and see the people inside the lounge and night club café. The room was glittering with gold trim and big chandeliers made out of lots of little pieces of hanging glass—the kind you see in pictures of rich people's homes.

Dodi Doll was singing in the night club, and her voice carried outside to where I was standing. She had a really good voice, with a lot of wham to it. She hardly needed the microphone. People clapped for her a lot when she finished the song, and she started a new one. I sat down in a deck chair that was back in the shadows, pulled the blanket up to my chin to keep warm, and listened to her sing. I wondered why she wanted to be a movie star when she could sing like that.

I heard footsteps coming along the deck from the stairway. Whoever it was took a few steps and then stopped, took a few more and stopped again, as though he were looking for someone or making sure he wasn't being watched.

I didn't even move. I just kept as still as I could while a dark shape came out of the shadows around the area between the stairway and the railing. There was enough light from the windows of the night club and the thin sliver of moon to show me who it was. With that big bushy beard, I would have known Mr. Riggle anywhere.

He didn't see me in the dark, which was good, because it was pretty obvious that he didn't want anyone to see him. He looked around, nervously, clutching a bundle, all wrapped up and lumpy where the string was tight. Then he reached far over the railing and threw the package into the water. The way it splashed I could tell it was weighted with something and pretty heavy.

He looked up and down the promenade again, then turned like a frightened rabbit and hurried out of sight in the direction of the stairway.

I knew I'd meet that guy, Riggle, again; but now I wondered what it was he'd been so secretive about throwing overboard. I still had a creepy feeling about that guy. What he had just done was awfully wrong. I shivered, and it wasn't because of the cold ocean air.

6

Mr. Riggle Disappears

I huddled under the blanket until I was sure that
Mr. Riggle had time to get far away. I didn't know
what to make of the guy. I didn't even know what
it was he had thrown overboard. Maybe it was just
something he got tired of carrying around with him
like, like . . . Gosh, I couldn't think of anything. It
was the way he did it, making such a big secret out
of it. That's what scared me so much. Something
mighty strange was going on.

The night breeze was getting pretty cold. I got up,
stretching and rubbing my arms to warm up, and went
inside the café to look at the clock. It was just a few
minutes after ten, so I went down one flight of stairs
to the upper deck and found the Handy's stateroom.

Wouldn't you know it, being all mixed up about
Mr. Riggle as I was, I knocked on the wrong door,
and Betty Frances opened it. She was sleepy, with her

hair all messed up and her robe twisted around her, and when she saw me she got mad.

"Why aren't you in bed?" she asked. She didn't even wait for an answer. She took me by one arm and marched me over to the next door. "You pull a stunt like this again, Frank Handy, and I'll tell your mother!"

Betty Frances knocked on the door, and one of the twins opened it a crack.

"Is that you, Joe?" he asked.

"Don't be funny," Betty Frances said. She pushed me inside and fumbled around for the light switch.

"Don't turn on the light," I whispered, fast as I could. "It will wake up the others."

"All right," she mumbled and yawned. "Do you promise me you'll go right to sleep?"

"I promise," I said.

She shut the door, and I gave a long sigh. Peter sat up in his bunk and turned on the light.

"Mom and Dad have already checked us."

I headed for the empty bunk, took off my shoes, and flopped down.

"Wait a minute," Peter said. "Harriet said for you to put on Frank's extra pajamas and brush your teeth."

I pulled the blankets over me. I was really beginning to get tired. "Harriet can go jump in the ocean," I said.

There was a gasp all around me.

"Harriet will kill you if she finds out."

"How's she going to find out?"

"She finds out everything," one of the twins said.

58

"Turn out the light," I said. "Let's get some sleep."

"Harriet knows judo," Peter said.

Frank raised his head from the pillow. "And karate."

"Turn out the light," I said again. "I'm tired."

One of the twins flicked the light switch, and I heard him jump back into bed.

"You're not afraid of Harriet?" Frank asked.

"Naw."

"He doesn't know Harriet very well," Peter said.

One of the twins chimed in, "Or else he's the bravest guy in the whole world."

Harriet sure had these guys under her thumb. I couldn't understand why they hadn't figured a few things out. I pulled my head out from under the blanket and said, "You know, if my sister knew judo and karate, I'd make it a point to learn them too."

I could hear four sets of wheels going around with every one of them thinking that over. I rolled on my stomach and went to sleep.

I hardly had time to finish one dream before Betty Frances was knocking on the door and telling us to get dressed for breakfast. The sunlight was spilling into the room. I swung over the edge of the bunk and sat there squinting and scratching my stomach.

Peter went over to Frank's bunk and pushed on his shoulder. "How do you feel, Frank?" he asked. "Are you still seasick?"

Frank raised his head. "I don't know yet," he said. "What is the boat doing?"

"It's moving," Peter said.

"I mean is it going up and down very much?"

At that moment we must have hit a big swell, because the ship gave a gentle rock back and forth.

I felt sorry for Frank. He really wasn't a bad guy, and anybody with Harriet for a twin didn't deserve to be seasick too. So I hopped up and said in a brisk voice, "It's a sunny day, and the sea is calm, and you'll feel great once you get a little exercise and a good breakfast inside you." I was willing to miss breakfast. My conscience hurt more than my stomach did.

"You think so?" Frank asked, looking hopeful.

The door banged open, and Harriet stuck her head inside, glaring at me. She must have been listening at the door.

"Oh, Frank," she said, "you know what's for breakfast? Those horrible fried eggs with the white all slimy and jellied looking, and the yolk kind of raw and staring up at you and looking gooey, and . . ."

Frank put his head under the pillow and groaned. "I don't want any breakfast," he said. "Everybody go away and leave me alone."

I slipped on my shoes and went out in the corridor with the other kids.

"You almost ruined everything," Harriet hissed at me.

"I felt sorry for him," I said.

"People who are escaping can't take time to feel sorry for anyone," she insisted. She stared at me as though she was nearsighted. "You're in the same messy clothes, and you didn't comb your hair."

"And he didn't. . . ," one of the twins started to

say, but Peter clapped his hand over the kid's mouth.

Harriet ignored him. "You can't go to breakfast with your hair a mess. Go comb it."

"Let's get one thing straight," I said, trying to look tough. "I don't let girls tell me what to do."

Harriet's mouth opened, and then she closed it, and gave me that same sneaky smile. "How would you like me to blow this whole thing for you?"

I shrugged. "Then you'd never find out from me what Mr. Riggle did last night when he thought no one was looking."

"What did he do?" She looked surprised.

"Say '*Please* comb you hair,' and I might tell you. Don't forget the *please*," I added.

Harriet began to look at me in a new way—as though I knew judo and karate too—and she said in a little voice, trying to sound sweet, "Please comb your hair, Joe."

"O.K.," I said. "I'll be right back."

I didn't use the bathroom in the stateroom because I hated to look at poor Frank again. I went down the hall to the men's room. I fished around in my slacks pockets and found a stub of a comb that I usually carry because Mrs. Crumbacher has a thing about hair combing too. When I started combing I leaned close to the mirror and a lot of sand fell out. The more I combed, the more came out, and it all fell in a pile on the ledge under the mirror. I poked it around with my finger, thinking that it came from Monday morning when I was playing touch football on the school playground and a bunch of us guys got to wrassling around in the sand box.

already, including Miss Stanhope, who still seemed to be upset.

Finally, when I was about ready to start squirming in my chair, Betty Frances said we could leave. She took the younger children to the playroom at the end of the upper deck and allowed the older ones to do what they wanted to do.

Harriet grabbed my arm and pulled me down a corridor and around a corner. "Now," she said, "tell me about Mr. Riggle."

Just then an officer rushed past us, not even noticing us and behind him were two ladies talking a mile a minute.

"Imagine that!" one of them said. "A man disappearing right from this ship."

"No one has found a single trace of him!"

"And nothing missing but the clothes he was wearing!"

Harriet and I looked at each other. I stepped out into the aisle just as they were passing us. "Pardon me, ma'am," I said. "Would you tell us about this man who is missing? We haven't heard what happened."

Even if we were just kids, the ladies were only too glad to have someone to tell their story to. They really didn't know much, just that Miss Stanhope had gone to the captain, upset because she couldn't find Mr. Riggle, and they had been looking all over the ship for him, and couldn't find him.

They hurried on their way, eager to run into someone else to tell, and for a moment Harriet and I didn't say anything.

65

Finally she peered at me out of the corners of her eyes and asked, "Did you do it?"

"Me? Of course I didn't."

"You're a logical suspect."

"Oh, get off it," I told her. "You watch too much television. How could I do anything to a big guy like that?"

"Is that what you were going to tell me?" Harriet asked. "About Mr. Riggle disappearing, I mean?"

"Look, Harriet," I said, "this is getting kind of serious. Let's go somewhere where no one can overhear us, and I'll tell you what happened last night. Maybe you and I can figure out what to do."

In spite of being a dumb girl, Harriet was really kind of smart, and at the moment I needed someone to talk to. Nearly everywhere we went there were people playing shuffleboard or taking a stroll or talking in groups, but we finally found a place at the very stern of the promenade deck where we could be alone. I told her about what I had seen, and she listened carefully.

"Are you sure it was Mr. Riggle?"

"Who else on this ship has a big bushy beard? I was close enough to him. I'm positive it was Mr. Riggle."

Harriet sighed. "And you can't tell the captain."

"I know it," I said. "If I did, it would get me in trouble, because I'm not supposed to be on the ship."

"And it doesn't really prove who the murderer is anyway," Harriet said.

"Murderer?"

"Look," Harriet started to explain. "Mr. Riggle

threw something overboard that somebody else wanted, so that somebody else threw Mr. Riggle overboard."

"That's pretty wild," I said.

"Can you think of anything better?"

For a few minutes I thought as hard as I could. "I guess not," I admitted.

"What should we do?"

I stood up and leaned against the rail, looking down into the water as though it could tell me something. "I think that we'd better not tell anyone about it just yet. We can keep watching people and see if we notice something else that might be suspicious."

Harriet looked excited. "Right!"

"I'll get Feef. It's time to take her for a walk."

"I'll go with you."

"No," I said. "You cover a different part of the ship. We'll discover more if we aren't together." I wasn't planning to spend any more time than I had to with Harriet.

Feef was as glad to see me as I was to see her. I slipped on her leash, and we took the elevator up to the promendade deck, and started going around and around. That sea air sure made me hungry. I was glad to see the guy with the big cart full of food again. We hurried over to him, and Feef sat down patiently, her tongue hanging out as she panted.

The guy gave me a funny look. "You again," he said. "Sorry there's no cake. In the morning we have hot soup."

"That's all right," I told him. "I eat anything."

I took a bowl of soup and half a dozen little buns

with ham in them and a couple of cinnamon rolls and sat down in a deck chair to enjoy a snack. One thing I had to say for this ship: It had a darned good cook on it. I thought I might even have seconds.

We were near the corridor to the inside stairway, and in a few minutes Miss Stanhope came bursting through, a bunch of ship's officers with her.

"We've looked everywhere! Everywhere! He's not on this ship!" Miss Stanhope began squeezing her hands together.

The officers were trying to calm her down, and she kept acting as though she were going to start bawling. Even poor little Feef got mixed up in the excitement because she hid under my deck chair and started growling at them. It was the first time I'd heard her growl at anyone.

I scooped Feef up in my arms and fed her the rest of my soup, which made her stop.

In a few minutes Miss Stanhope and the officers disappeared down the corridor again. Feef wiped the rest of the soup off of her nose with a swipe of her tongue and gave one last snarl.

"What's got into you, Feef?" I asked. "You have better manners than that."

She licked my cheek, which I took to be an apology.

"How about some more soup?" I asked, but I looked up to find the guy with the cart glaring at me. I just put down my empty bowl and plate and walked Feef up to the sun deck where we could watch people play badminton.

We stayed there, enjoying the warm sun, until Feef

caught one of the birdies and pulled the feathers out, and some sorehead asked us to leave.

We got into the elevator, and a couple of people joined us. They were talking about the mysterious disappearance of Mr. Riggle.

"They found a clue," the woman was saying as the door closed and the elevator began to move slowly downward.

"What was it?" the man asked.

"A strange design made of sand in the shape of an arrow. It was on the shelf in the men's room on the upper deck."

"That was a clue?"

"It was pointing toward the porthole," she said, almost whispering. "They think it was poor Mr. Riggle's last attempt to tell the world that someone was throwing him overboard."

She put her hand over her mouth and looked kind of scared. They got off at the next deck, and Feef and I rode down to the main deck alone.

Oh boy! I thought. One more complication. This guy Riggle—wherever he was, or *wasn't*—had started to haunt me!

7

Another Mistake

After lunch I went to the upper deck again. I thought I'd tell Dodi Doll that I was taking good care of Feef. I went up the stairway and around the corridor just in time to see Miss Stanhope slip into a door close to Dodi's. It looked as though it might be next door to hers.

When I got to Dodi's door I knocked lightly and heard her call out, "Come in."

She was dressed in a purple slacks outfit and lying on top of her bed with a washcloth over her forehead.

"Are you sick?" I asked.

She held up one corner of the washcloth and peeked out at me. "Oh, it's you, Joe. Hello. No, I'm not sick. I'm just tired."

"I guess they keep you working late at night."

"It isn't that so much," she said. "It's all the practicing Jerry makes me do. I have to keep reading

Romeo and Juliet over and over until I'm sick of it."

"Why do you have to do that?"

She sighed. "Jerry said I'm a terrible actress and need all the practice I can get if I ever hope to become a movie star."

"Maybe it's the script he gave you," I told her. "My dad says that a lot of good actors are ruined by terrible scripts."

She sat up on the bed and smiled at me. "Do you think so, really?"

"Why not?"

She put down the washcloth and looked as though she felt a lot better.

"I heard you sing last night," I told her. "It was real good. Maybe you should be a singer instead of a movie star."

Dodi got a big smile on her face. "I think I'd like to go on being a singer. But Jerry tells me that there's a lot more future in being a movie star." She got up and wandered over to the mirror, where she took a good look at herself. Then she turned around and put her hands on my shoulders.

"I've never had any really nice things," she told me. "You know, like diamonds and mink coats and big cars—all of that. Jerry says if I get to be a movie star I'll have all of those that I want."

"Yeah," I said. "I guess I understand."

I really didn't. I thought it would be a lot nicer to do what you wanted to do instead of what some other guy thought you should do.

"You're a nice kid, Joe," Dodi said. "Wish me luck."

I suddenly remembered seeing Miss Stanhope in the

71

hall. "Did you hear about that guy named Mr. Riggle disappearing last night?" I asked Dodi.

"Sure," she said. "Everybody's heard about it. They had to wire back to the States and inform his company."

"A little while ago I saw his secretary go in a door close to yours."

"That must have been Miss Stanhope." Dodi wrinkled her nose. "She certainly has thick ankles."

I wondered what was the matter with girls that their minds worked in such crazy ways. I guess I never was going to be able to understand them.

"Miss Stanhope's stateroom is right next to mine." Dodi said. "And Mr. Riggle's was next to hers, poor man. Do you think he fell overboard?"

"I guess so." I couldn't imagine Mr. Riggle still being on the ship. There weren't that many places to hide, believe me, and there were too many people around checking into all those places.

There was a knock at the door, and I jumped. "I'd better get going," I told her. "I just wanted to let you know that Feef was coming along fine."

"Feef who?"

"Feef—the little dog, the blue dog you asked me to take care of."

Her eyes lit up. "Oh, yes. The dog."

"She likes me a lot."

"So do I, Joe," she said.

It was all right with me the way she said it. Some girls would say a thing like that all gooey and make you feel sick to your stomach. But Dodi was different. She just said it and meant it, and that was that.

I opened the door, and Jerry barged right past me. He was waving a script and shouting that they'd have to practice some more, and he slammed the door without even saying hello.

Out in the corridor I saw Harriet charging toward me, her arms waving like a windmill. I could probably have outrun her, but I thought she might know something I'd want to hear. I waited for her to catch up.

"Boy, am I glad I found you!" she yelled. "Betty Frances sent me looking for you. She wants us all to meet in the theater."

"Theater? Do they have movies on this ship?"

"They do tonight, but that's not the reason. They're having a talent show on Friday, and Mom told Betty Frances that she wants all of us to sing something. Ever since she saw *The Sound of Music*, she thinks we're another Trapp family."

"Are you any good?"

Harriet shrugged and tried to look modest. "Some of the younger ones aren't too hot, but Frank's pretty good, and I'm practically professional."

She didn't give me time to answer, which is too bad, because I was going to let go with an awful insult I learned from a kid on my block named Al. But she kept chattering away until we got to the theater on the promenade deck.

Betty Frances was trying to get the others to stay in a straight line. She looked up when we came in and said, "Thank goodness. Now we can begin. I thought I'd go out of my mind before you got here."

Betty Frances shoved us into the back row. "Now,"

she said, "we'll start with that Mexican folk song your mother likes so much."

"What folk song?" I whispered to Harriet.

She hummed a few bars under her breath, and I was relieved that I knew it. It was one we had learned in school.

"Pay attention!" Betty Frances hummed a note until we all got it and said, "Hit it!"

We sang one verse—or at least they sang, and I faked it. Then Betty Frances stopped swinging her hands long enough to point one finger at me and call, "Step forward, Frank, and solo."

"Me?" I gulped.

"Go ahead," she said.

I ought to get credit for the way I tried. It's just that I had forgotten to tell Harriet one thing. I'm tone deaf. When everyone else is singing along with the notes, I'm singing someplace else. It's not my fault, and sometimes I get a music teacher who feels sorry for me and doesn't give me a "D."

All of them stopped, and Betty Frances made a face. "Your mother told me you sing like an angel. How biased can parents get!"

"Want me to try it over?"

"No thanks!" She looked at the rest of them. "Can any of you do better than Frank?"

"I can," Harriet said.

So she got up in front and did the solo and sounded all right, I guess, although I hate to admit it. And I just went back to faking it in the last row.

I could hardly get Harriet off my neck the rest of the day. She even tagged along when I walked Feef

74

after dinner. It wasn't so bad in the movie, though, because I didn't have to look at her. As far as being detectives and trying to find out what happened to Mr. Riggle, we were terrible. We couldn't think of anything and didn't turn up with a single clue.

The next morning Harriet was still giving Frank the business to keep him seasick. I thought by now he'd be sick enough of the bouillon soup she kept bringing him.

At breakfast, though, we found there was another mystery on board. Dodi Doll's agent had announced to the captain that someone had stolen her diamond necklace, the one she had worn in her night club show.

The whole thing seemed strange to me. From the way Dodi had talked, I didn't think she had a diamond necklace. The more I tried to figure things out, the more I decided to go and see Dodi and ask her about it.

I sneaked away from Harriet after breakfast while she was busy bossing her brothers and sisters around, and went down to the kennels to get Feef. After we got through greeting each other, and I dried off my face, I walked her up to Dodi's stateroom and knocked on the door.

The door next to hers opened a crack, and Miss Stanhope's face peered out.

"I thought you were knocking on my door," she mumbled.

"No, ma'am," I said. "Sorry if we bothered you."

But Feef took one look at Miss Stanhope, bared her teeth, and let loose with a growl.

"Hey, Feef!" I picked her up and started to apolo-

gize for her bad manners, but Miss Stanhope had shut
the door. "Why do you want to act like that?" I said
to Feef. "I thought you were a nice dog."

Feef gave a little whimper and slobbered down my
neck.

Dodi Doll's door opened just then, and she said,
"Hi, Joe. Come on in."

Jerry was there too, but he was getting ready to
leave. "I don't know if we're getting enough publicity
on it," he said. "It's hard to tell if the wire services
have picked it up or not—at least until we get the
evening news."

He left, and I said, "I'm sorry about your necklace
being stolen. I didn't know you had a diamond
necklace."

Dodi didn't hear me. She grabbed up an eyeglass
case and ran to the door with it. She stuck her head
in the hall and looked both ways, then came back and
handed it to me.

"Will you do me a favor, Joe? Jerry is blind as a
bat without his reading glasses, and he gets so mad
when he discovers that he left them someplace. Will
you take these to his stateroom?"

She gave me the number, which was at the end of
the corridor, and I walked Feef down there. The door
was open, and the maid was cleaning up, but Jerry
wasn't there.

"I have to put these glasses on the dresser," I ex-
plained.

"Go ahead," she said, and went back to her cart in
the corridor to get some more stuff.

I put Feef down, which was a mistake, because she

76

kept sniffing around, the way dogs do in strange places. There was a coat on the edge of a chair, and she caught it in her teeth and pulled it to the floor, worrying it the way she would a rabbit.

"You know better than that, Feef," I said. I took the coat away from her, but I grabbed it upside down, and something fell out of the pocket and landed on the rug. It was a necklace.

I picked it up and took a good look. It didn't look like a diamond necklace to me. It looked more like one of those rhinestone things, but I decided I didn't know much about jewelry. Anyhow, it struck me as a lucky break for Dodi that I had come down here. Jerry had probably put her necklace in his pocket and forgotten all about it, and that's why they thought it was stolen! Boy, would they be happy when I brought it back!

I grabbed Feef and nearly ran down the corridor to Dodi's room. The door was open, and Jerry was back, and so was the ship's captain.

I held the necklace up high and waved it at them. "Look!" I shouted. "I found it! It wasn't stolen after all!"

Dodi's mouth opened wide, and then she said, "Thank you, Joe," in a funny little voice that didn't sound like hers.

The captain looked at each of us in turn. "It's fortunate that the boy found the necklace," he said. "It saves us a lot of embarrassing publicity." He stalked out of the room and was out of sight before anybody could say anything.

"I'm gonna throw that kid to the sharks!" Jerry

77

shouted as he started after me, but Dodi grabbed him and pushed him out the door, saying, "Oh, Jerry, he was trying to help! He was just trying to help!"

She shut the door and stood with her back to it, shaking her head at me. "I should think that your father would have told you about publicity stunts," she said.

"You mean losing your necklace was a publicity stunt?"

"No, having it stolen was."

"Why?"

"Don't ask me. Jerry said that movie stars are always getting their jewelry stolen. They get lots of publicity that way."

"I think it's kind of silly," I said.

She thought for a minute. "I guess it is. But Jerry said it was the thing to do."

There was a loud knocking at the door. "Get that kid outa there!" Jerry yelled.

Dodi patted my shoulder. "I'll take care of Jerry. You just leave—fast."

She opened the door and hung onto Jerry, trying to pull him into the stateroom, while Feef and I lit out in a hurry. I didn't know why I was always getting into trouble. Especially when I was trying extra hard to do something nice.

8

A Pair of Spies

Feef and I went up to the promenade deck because that seemed to be the place she liked best. The people there, for the most part, were friendly people and were busy talking while they strolled around or rested in those big deck chairs. A lot of them still stared at Feef, but she didn't seem to mind as long as I was with her. It's a nice feeling to have a dog crazy about you. I guess it comes second to parents.

We hadn't been on deck long before I realized something was going on in back of me. Every now and then I caught a flash of red hair, and from the corners of my eyes I could see that Harriet was shadowing me. I'd go a few steps, and so would she. I'd stop at the rail, and she'd flatten herself against the side of the ship.

I pretended that I hadn't seen her and casually

strolled into the corridor leading to the stairway. I didn't have to wait there long. Harriet came rushing around the corner, nearly bumping into us.

"What are you doing, knucklehead?" I asked her.

"I wanted to see what you were doing," she said.

"You're not supposed to spy on me."

"I couldn't find anyone else to spy on."

She stooped and patted Feef's head. "She's a nice dog," she said. "I wonder if she minds being blue."

"It will grow out."

Feef got real friendly with Harriet, which made me wonder if Feef was as smart as I had thought she was. Harriet liked Feef too.

"Is she this friendly with everyone?" she asked.

"Just about," I said. Then I remembered the way Feef had acted with Miss Stanhope.

"Except for one person," I added. "She keeps growling at Miss Stanhope, and I can't figure out why."

"That's funny," Harriet said. "Has Miss Stanhope ever been mean to Feef?"

"I don't think so. Feef acted like that the first time she saw Miss Stanhope."

"We had a dog once," Harriet said. "She used to try to bite the paper boy, and we found out later that he had hit her with a stick."

"I don't blame the dog."

"Me either," Harriet said. "I got so mad when I found out, I wanted to bite the paper boy myself."

"He probably would have got rabies," I said.

Harriet stuck her tongue out at me and went on

81

talking. I guess she was used to getting insulted by her brothers.

"Has anybody ever hurt Feef?" she asked. "I think we ought to investigate this."

"Yeah. That Mr. Riggle did. We bumped into him, going around a corner, the first day on the ship. He kicked Feef."

"We might have a clue there."

"How?" I asked. "Just because Mr. Riggle kicked her doesn't mean Feef would get mad at his secretary too."

Harriet stood up and looked thoughtful. "You know, Joe, something strange is going on."

"I know it," I said.

"Don't you think Miss Stanhope is kind of a peculiar person?"

I hadn't given it much thought, but I decided Harriet was right. I nodded my head.

Harriet's voice got low and sneaky. "We could shadow her and see if she's up to anything."

"Not the way you shadowed me," I told her. "You go about it all wrong."

"I suppose you know so much!"

I looked her straight in the eye. "How old are you?" I asked.

She blinked a couple of times. "Ten and a half."

"When you're as old as I am," I said, "you'll have learned a few things, and one of them is not to go leaping and ducking around when you're following someone. You give yourself away right off the bat."

Harriet looked impressed, which is saying a lot for a

girl like her. "O.K., know-it-all. How do you go about it?"

"Lesson number one," I said. "You don't sneak, and you don't hide. You just stroll along as though you weren't paying attention to anybody, but you manage to keep a sharp eye on your suspect."

Harriet clapped her hands together. "Can we do it?"

"All right," I said. "But if you get the least bit silly or start acting like a dumb girl, you're fired."

It took us awhile to find Miss Stanhope. Harriet went down to double-check her stateroom, in case she was holed up in there, and I covered the top decks. I was finishing a search of the boat deck, when I looked down from the balcony over the swimming pool area and saw that the buffet lunch was being served.

I realized that I had been so busy I had forgotten about the guy with the cart and had missed my morning snack. I was ready to drop the whole bit with Harriet and Miss Stanhope when I noticed that Miss Stanhope was holding a plate and standing in line near the buffet table. There was something puzzling about her, but I couldn't put my finger on it.

Harriet came into sight just then and nodded at me very importantly which meant that she was watching Miss Stanhope too. I had a good view from the balcony, but I was too far away from the food, and it really looked good. I led Feef downstairs and stood on the outer edge of the crowd. Some people took their plates and sat down near me, but I just stood there with Feef, keeping an eye on Miss Stanhope. Harriet got a plate and really heaped it up, which I thought was pretty mean since I was willing to stand there and starve; but it just went to prove that girls make rotten spies.

All of a sudden the man sitting next to me let out a shout, and I turned around to find that Feef had eaten the man's lunch while he was busy talking to the lady beside him. The man probably didn't feel too well, because he got awfully crabby about the whole thing. I took Feef down to the kennels.

When I came back I couldn't find Harriet. Miss Stanhope was sitting by herself. I walked up to get my plate and then looked around for Harriet again. I was passing a deck chair, when a voice said, "Psst, Joe. Sit down here—next to me."

There was Harriet lying in a deck chair with a newspaper over her face, looking like someone who had gone to sleep in the sun. Only she had made two little holes in the paper to look through. At a distance it was all right, but if you looked closely it was creepy, because one hole was poked right into the face of a horse, and here was this blue eye going around and around.

"That's a crazy trick," I told her, sitting down.

"Talk out of the corner of your mouth," she said, "so no one will know you're talking to me."

"I will not," I said. "I'm not going to talk at all. I'm going to eat. I'm hungry."

"Then I'll talk to you," she said. And wouldn't you know it, the first thing she said was a question, so I had to answer.

"Are you sure you weren't telling a big, big fib about Mr. Riggle throwing something overboard?"

I was so surprised I stopped eating. "Why do you ask a dumb question like that? I was telling the truth."

The newspaper nodded up and down. "All right then," she said. "That just makes everything more suspicious."

"Why?"

"Because," she said, "I overheard Miss Stanhope telling one of the ship's officers that not a thing of Mr. Riggle's was missing, except the clothes he was wearing."

"That's strange," I said.

"You don't suppose he could have been . . . well, standing at the rail with nothing on, throwing his clothes overboard?"

"Harriet!" I said, "Don't you think that's something I would have noticed?"

"It was just a wild guess."

"It sure was."

I went on eating, and for a long time Harriet was quiet, which was a real miracle. I finished the last bite and put down my plate.

"Do you understand grownups?" I asked her.

"No," she said. "Why?"

"They do the darndest things. Here Dodi Doll was hiding something real and insisting it was missing when it wasn't, and Miss Stanhope is insisting nothing is missing when something is."

"What is?" she asked.

"Whatever was in the package."

A shadow fell across the newspaper, and I looked up

to see Miss Stanhope going past us. She didn't pause, but she looked at me with pure hatred in her eyes. It was such an awful look that it scared me. Why should she stare at me like that? Had she overheard what I'd said about the package?

9

A Dangerous Trick

I got Feef out of the kennels again in the afternoon. The guy in the kennels was real friendly, and we talked for awhile, and I played with Feef. Then I took her back up to the promenade deck. I saw Dodi Doll in a deck chair. As Jerry wasn't anywhere around, I sat down in the chair next to hers.

She had on big dark glasses and looked like a movie star already. I told her so.

"You're the nicest boy I ever met," she said, reaching out to pat my hand. "Are you having fun on this cruise? What have you been doing?"

"I've been feeling sorry that I spoiled your publicity stunt," I apologized. "I didn't mean to."

She gave a little laugh. "Oh, that's all right. I don't mind. Jerry is working on a new one."

"What is it?" I asked. "Better tell me, so I won't mess it up too."

"You can't with this one. Jerry is wiring the newspapers that I'm going to South America to meet Robert Vaughn and marry him."

"You are?" I nearly jumped out of my chair. I didn't like the idea of Dodi getting married.

"Oh, not really. I told you it was a publicity stunt. You see, after all the newspapers print that I'm going to marry Robert Vaughn, Jerry wires then again that I'm quite upset at the rumor and I hotly deny it. That way I get my name in the newspapers twice."

"It sounds crazy to me."

"It does to me too, but Jerry says that all the movie stars do it."

A woman came along the deck and stopped at the foot of Dodi's deck chair.

"Are you Dodi Doll, the singer?" She kind of gurgled as she talked, and had a silly smile on her face.

"Yes, I am," Dodi said.

The woman rummaged through her purse and came up with a pencil and a piece of paper. "Oh, could I have your autograph?" she asked.

"I'd be delighted," Dodi said. She signed her name with a couple of extra flourishes and handed the paper and pencil back to the woman.

"Oh, thank you!" the woman said. "I'm going to write and tell my sister in Omaha that I met you."

The woman scurried off, and Dodi watched her go. "Someday, when I'm a famous movie star, people are going to ask for my autograph," she said.

"Somebody just did," I told her. "That woman thought you were famous already."

Dodi looked surprised, then grinned.

"Why can't you be a famous singer instead of a

famous movie star?" I asked her. "Especially if you like singing best?"

Just then' old Harriet came bouncing down the promenade and started tugging at my arm.

"Who's your girl friend?" Dodi asked me.

Girl friend! I nearly got sick to my stomach, especially when Harriet giggled, but I had to introduce Harriet.

"Miss Stanhope is down in her stateroom now," Harriet said, bobbing her head up and down and winking at me.

"Why are you tailing her?" Dodi asked.

"Harriet!" I said. "You see how dumb you are? You give everything away!"

Harriet ignored me and turned to Dodi. "There's something strange about her. Even Feef doesn't like her."

"I don't think Feef likes me either," Dodi said.

"That's different," Harriet said. "She doesn't growl at you, but she growls at Miss Stanhope."

"That's funny," Dodi said. "Maybe she just doesn't like Miss Stanhope's looks."

"Miss Stanhope really is ugly," Harriet said.

"She wears her dresses too long," Dodi said, "and funny, flat-heeled shoes."

"And her ankles are thick and knobby."

"They certainly are," Dodi said. "I noticed her ankles right away. I've never seen a woman with such ugly ankles. They look more like a man's."

Harriet blabbed on, but I stopped listening. I wondered if either of them had paid attention to what

they had said. I was beginning to get an idea from
Dodi's remark about Miss Stanhope's ankles, and I
had to talk to Harriet right away.

This time *I* tugged on *her* arm. "Come on," I said.
"Dodi needs to get some rest. She has a show tonight."

I got Harriet away from there as fast as I could,
pulling her with one hand and Feef with the other
until we were in a quiet corner in the writing room,
which was the first room we came to. Luckily the
room was almost empty.

I pushed Harriet into a chair and sat down next
to her.

"What's the matter with you?" she asked.

"I think you and Dodi discovered something important," I told her. "Remember when you were talking about how horrible Miss Stanhope looked? Dodi
said her ankles looked like a man's instead of a
woman's."

I let Harriet think this over for a few minutes, and
I could see her little brain churning around under
that fuzzy red hair.

"Then," Harriet said finally, "that means that Miss
Stanhope could be a man in disguise."

"Right," I said, "and he could be holding the real
Miss Stanhope and Mr. Riggle prisoner in Miss Stanhope's stateroom."

Harriet clutched my arm. "Or he could have thrown
them overboard."

I nodded.

"We'd better tell the captain," Harriet whispered.

"How can we? We aren't really positive. It would

cause a real mess if we insisted that Miss Stanhope was a man in disguise, and we were wrong. We might even get into trouble."

"What do we do?"

"We're going to have to prove Miss Stanhope is a man. If he is a man, he'll be wearing a woman's wig. That's what we have to find out."

Harriet looked at her watch. "Better take Feef back, and we can think about what to do. We've got to show up at the theater for some more practice in a few minutes or Betty Frances will come looking for us." She shook her head. "You know, you sing worse than anybody I ever heard in my life."

If she weren't a girl I would have taken a poke at her, but instead I had to promise to meet her at the theater. I walked Feef back to the kennels.

The rehearsal went about as badly as before, and I wondered if the audience would groan and boo when we finished singing on Friday night, or if they would be polite. I know what I would have done.

We stopped back at the staterooms because Betty Frances had some notion we should clean up before dinner. Frank was sitting on his bunk. He looked a little pale, but a lot better.

"I think I might come to dinner," he said to Harriet.

"You're lucky," she said, without batting an eye. "Tonight is a special French dinner. They're going to start out with snails."

"Snails?" Frank said, a funny look on his face.

"Yes," she said. "All Frenchmen love to eat snails. They take them out of the shells, and after they're

through squirming and wiggling around all slimy and
sticky, they boil them. When they're sure they're dead,
they serve them with lots of butter so you can gulp
them down fast and not be able to tell if there's a
slippery wiggle or two left in them."

"Ugh!" Frank said. He lay down again.

"Would you rather I brought you some of that
bouillon soup?"

"Go away," Frank mumbled. "I don't want anything!" He looked up at us for a moment and
promised, "When I feel better I'm going to clobber
both of you!"

We went out in the corridor, and Harriet said, "It
would have been terrible if Frank came to dinner. You
need to be in the dining room with me when Miss
Stanhope comes in."

"So we can find out if she's wearing a wig," I
added.

Miss Stanhope had already arrived in the dining
room and was busy eating when we came to our
table. Betty Frances made the usual clucking noises,
attempting to get everyone seated, but Harriet and I
kept trying to stare at Miss Stanhope without getting
caught at it.

"I can't tell from here," Harriet said.

"I can't tell anyway," I told her. "How do you know
what a wig looks like?"

"If I could get a close look," Harriet said, "I think
I'd know."

"How are you going to manage that?"

Harriet pointed at a waiter who was standing in

93

back of Miss Stanhope's table, and then she carefully dropped her fork under the table.

She slid her chair back. "I'll go over and ask the waiter for another fork. I'll have to go right past Miss Stanhope."

But Betty Frances was too quick for us. "Where are you going, Harriet?" she asked.

"To ask the waiter for another fork. Mine fell."

"Sit down," Betty Frances ordered, handing her a fork. "You can use Amy's. She eats everything with a spoon."

"Think of something else," I whispered.

"Like what?"

The waiter placed large plates of tossed salad in front of us and left to serve the next table.

"Why don't you drop some food on your dress?" I asked. "Then you'll have to leave to change."

Harriet beamed. "You're positively brilliant!"

Everything that girl did, she did too much of. She had a lot to learn. She proceeded to dump the whole salad plate into her lap.

"Really, Harriet," Betty Frances said, acting upset. "At your age you should have better table manners than that. I don't know which one of you is the sloppiest—you or Frank."

I chuckled a little to myself until I realized that she thought I was Frank. I couldn't imagine why she thought I was sloppy. I decided she didn't like me because I couldn't sing.

Harriet finished picking the lettuce and tomatoes off her lap. "I've got to change my dress," she said.

94

"Wait until after dinner," Betty Frances said.

"But I'm all messy, and I can't stand looking messy!"

"You might spill something again."

"No, I won't. I promise! Please let me change my dress!"

Betty Frances gave a big sigh. "Well, hurry back."

Harriet took an out-of-the-way route from the dining room, right by the back of Miss Stanhope's hair. Luckily, Miss Stanhope didn't notice her. In a few minutes she returned in a clean dress, passed Miss Stanhope again, and came to the table shaking her head.

"It looks like a wig, but I can't be positive," she whispered to me.

The waiter had removed the salad plates and had brought the main course. Harriet sat down, bumping the edge of the table and knocking a slice of roast beef with gravy into her lap.

"Oh, Harriet!" Betty Frances moaned.

Harriet tried to smile sweetly. "I don't mind," she said. "It feels warm. It's quite comfortable."

"But now you've ruined another dress." While Betty Frances was busy taking peas away from Amy, who was throwing them, one by one, at John, Harriet put the slice of beef back on her plate, cut it up, and began to eat it.

"Is there any way we can find out for sure if that's a wig?" I asked her. "You know more about girls' things than I do."

Harriet started talking with her mouth full, which

made her mumble. "She'd have to take off that wig sometime, wouldn't she?"

"When would that be?"

"At night, when she's asleep, or in the bathtub." She gave a big gulping swallow. "You can't get them wet in the bathtub."

"Or in the swimming pool!"

"If Miss Stanhope is somebody else in disguise, she's not going to take off her wig to go swimming. Are you crazy?"

"No," I said. "The trick is to get her into that swimming pool without her suspecting anything."

Harriet stopped eating and stared at me. "How can we do that?"

"It's easy," I said. "We can try it after dinner. We'll stand outside her door, and you can pretend to rush up and find me there and tell me that you've discovered Mr. Riggle in the swimming pool, and no one else knows about it, and what should you do? And I can tell you to get the captain."

"And out of curiosity she'll come to the pool?"

"Right," I said. "And I'll push her in. And if she's wearing a wig it will float."

"You're terribly clever," Harriet said with a sigh.

Miss Stanhope pushed her chair back and stood up. I grabbed Harriet's shoulder and gave her a shove. "Follow her," I said, "and make sure she goes to her stateroom."

"What if she doesn't?"

"Just stick with her. I'll find you wherever you go."

Harriet jumped up, and Betty Frances said, "What in the world? Where are you going now, Harriet?"

"My dress is a mess!" Harriet said. "I've got to change it right now!"

"But . . ." Whatever it was Betty Frances wanted to say, she was too late, because Harriet was practically out of sight, hot on Miss Stanhope's trail.

"I think," Betty Frances said very slowly and carefully, taking Amy's hand out of a dish of jello, "that sooner or later I shall go out of my mind!"

Dinner seemed to take an awfully long time. I ate Harriet's dessert too because I didn't have anything else to do. Finally, Betty Frances excused us, and I hurried to the upper deck.

I was very careful going around corners. I didn't want to run into either Miss Stanhope or Jerry. I poked my head around the corridor leading from the elevators, and there was Harriet stationed outside Miss Stanhope's door. When she saw me she signaled frantically.

I walked as quietly as I could to join her, and she whispered, "She went right to her stateroom. She's in there now."

"I'll check around the pool," I said. "It's dark outside; it should be deserted."

I raced up the stairs to the promenade deck. The folding doors to the deck café, which overlooked the pool, had been closed to protect people from the chilly night winds, and the area around the pool was empty.

As fast as I could, I dashed back to Harriet, who was standing on one foot and then on the other, like a stork.

"Where were you?" she asked. "I got tired of waiting."

97

"I had to make sure no one was there. Are you ready?"

Harriet nodded and tiptoed to the end of the corridor. Then, like a herd of elephants, she came charging down the hallway. Miss Stanhope couldn't help hearing her.

"Joe!" she yelled in anguish, hamming it up. I knew Harriet would ham it up. "Joe, I have seen a most fiendish sight!"

"What was it?" I yelled back.

"Oh, the horror of it!" she cried out.

"Harriet, honest to Pete, will you . . ." I whispered, but she went right on, making a face at me.

"I have seen Mr. Riggle floating in the pool. What shall I do? What shall I do?"

"Was anyone else at the pool?"

"No one!" She yelled even more loudly, "The pool is deserted!"

"I'll go to the captain with you!" I said.

"Let's hurry then because it will probably take us about fifteen minutes to find him!"

Just then a door burst open, but it was Dodi's door. "I heard what you said," she gasped. "I'll go to the pool while you go for the captain."

I pulled her back into her stateroom and pulled Harriet in with us. "No," I whispered. "Mr. Riggle isn't really in the swimming pool. We're suspicious of Miss Stanhope, because . . . well, it's a long story. We're just trying to trap her. I'll explain everything to you later."

Just then we heard the tiny click of a door opening, and a second click as it shut. Harriet opened Dodi's

98

door just a crack, peeked out, and nodded to us. "It's Miss Stanhope all right. She's going down the hall as fast as she can!"

"We've got to go," I said to Dodi. "I'll tell you about it when we find out what we want to find out."

Harriet and I banged into each other trying to get out of the door at the same time, both of us knocking into the corridor walls and making a terrible racket.

We took the other stairway and circled around the far end of the pool, creeping as we got closer. Miss Stanhope was standing at one end of the pool, looking down into the water. I guess she was too anxious to be aware of us coming closer and closer to her, because I got right up to her before she heard me. She started to turn around, but she tripped over my foot and fell into the pool.

There was just one problem. She fell feet first, and I didn't realize that we happened to be standing by the shallow end of the pool, so that the water only came up to her waist. Her wig stayed right on her head.

I wasn't thinking very fast, I guess, because I should have lit out of there in a hurry, but I didn't move, and that gave Miss Stanhope time to grab my leg and pull me in too.

I went under and came up gasping for air, with Miss Stanhope doing her best to push me under again. There was something I had forgotten to tell Harriet.

"Harriet!" I managed to yell while I tried to fight off Miss Stanhope. "Harriet! I can't swim!"

Down I went another time, and I kicked and hit out as hard as I could. Miss Stanhope's chin rubbed

99

against my arm, and that was proof enough for me. I never heard of a lady with a stubbly rough chin.

Just when I thought I was going to explode, I was able to fight upward, into the air, gasping for breath. At that moment Harriet threw one of the heavy life-saver rings hanging around the pool and clipped Stanhope right on the forehead.

She staggered back a few steps, stunned for the moment, and I broke free.

Harriet jumped up and down and shouted like crazy, "Run, Joe! Run! Run!"

10

Joe on the Run

It's awfully hard to run in water. It feels like you're stuck in the middle of a slow motion movie. But I managed to make it to the side of the pool away from Stanhope. I scrambled over the side and stood there, gulping in the air, trying to get my breath back.

Behind me I heard Harriet give a little shriek and scream, "Run, Joe! She's coming after you!"

I took a look over my shoulder and saw that Stanhope was charging through the water toward me like an angry bull moose. Harriet was already running toward the right side of the promenade deck. I hurried toward the left.

I was dripping wet and leaving a nice trail of water behind me. I dashed into the club room, hoping the rug would soak up the wet spots so they wouldn't be so noticeable. I had to dodge between groups of people, who all looked at me kind of funny, but I didn't care. I just wanted to lose Stanhope in a hurry.

A couple of times I stopped to glance over my shoulder, but I wasn't able to see much with all the people around. I decided my best bet was to get to the Handy stateroom. Just as I dashed into the main lounge the elevator doors opened, and I ran in with the rest of the people.

The elevator doors closed, and I sighed with relief. For a few minutes I was safe. I relaxed against a lady who said, "Issh!" or something like that, and pulled away from me. It's odd how fussy some people can be about a few drops of water. It was nice clean water too.

I forgot to tell the operator I wanted to get off at the upper deck. She didn't stop and went all the way down to the main deck, where most of the people seemed to be going for dinner. I should have ridden that elevator right back up to the upper deck, I guess, but I saw Jerry standing on the edge of a group of people waiting for the elevator, so I sneaked behind the last person to get out and scurried around the corner. Where to now? I was stuck!

Right in front of my nose was a door with a sign, "Ship's Doctor." I stepped inside to give myself a chance to work out a plan. Nobody would think of looking for me there.

A nice-looking guy in an officer's uniform was sitting on top of the desk clipping his fingernails.

He looked up when I came in. "Fall in the swimming pool?"

"Yeah," I said, sort of surprised. "How did you know?"

"Simple matter of deduction," he said. "If you fell overboard, they'd have sounded an alarm, and not many people take a shower with their clothes on."

I gave an embarrassed laugh and said, "I should have thought of that."

"I'll give you some vitamin C pills to ward off a cold, and you get into some dry clothes in a hurry."

"Are you the doctor?"

"That's right," he said. "And not a very busy one either because people who take cruises are almost always in the best of health. My job usually consists of giving people Dramamine for sea sickness when we hit rough weather."

He went to a cabinet, poured a couple of pills into his hand, and gave them to me with a glass of water.

As I swallowed them my brain was spinning like sixty. Here was a chance to get protection all the way back to the Handy stateroom. If Stanhope saw me, he wouldn't dare chase me with a ship's officer right by my side.

"I've got a brother Frank who's awfully seasick," I told him. "But I don't know if your pills will work because my sister Harriet says it's all in his mind."

"Dramamine will work anyway," he said, "but I'd have to see your brother. I can't just hand out medicine without knowing if it's what is really needed. Better bring Frank down here."

"The last time I saw him, he said he was too sick to get out of bed. Could you come up to our stateroom?"

The doctor took another bottle of pills out of the

cabinet and put them into a small black bag. "Let's go," he said.

We went to the elevator and up to the next deck. All the way to the Handy stateroom I kept right by the doctor's side, and I looked around for a glimpse of Stanhope. I thought once that I saw him down at the end of the corridor, but whoever had been standing there disappeared as we got closer.

I opened the door to the boys' stateroom and led the doctor inside. Harriet was sitting on one of the bunks, telling Peter and Frank about Stanhope. The little kids must have been with Betty Frances.

Harriet jumped up when she saw me. "You're safe!" she yelled.

The doctor looked at Harriet, then at me, and back to Harriet. "Did you think he had drowned?" he asked her.

"Oh, no," she said. "He fell in the shallow end. The water only came up to his armpits."

"Then why were you worried about him?"

Harriet looked at me. I frowned and shook my head. I didn't want her to blab the whole story to this doctor."

"Well," she said, "He can't swim."

The doctor shrugged. "It makes about as much sense as anything else I've heard today." He turned to me. "Which is the sick boy?"

I pointed to Frank, and the doctor squatted on the floor in front of him, opening his black bag. "You," he said, waving a tongue depressor at me, "change your wet clothes right now!"

Harriet realized that I didn't know where Frank's

clothes would be, so she ran over to the dresser and took out some underwear, a knit shirt, and a pair of slacks. "Let me help you, dear brother," she said in a sicky-sweet voice.

I took the clothes and went into the bathroom to change. Frank didn't notice what we were doing because he had his mouth wide open with the tongue depressor halfway down his throat.

"You look all right," the doctor said. "Just tell me how you feel."

I shut the door and changed clothes in a hurry. I wondered if that medicine the doctor told me about would really cure Frank. I was beginning to get hungry just thinking about all the meals I was going to miss.

When I came back into the stateroom, the doctor was leaving. "I'll give the rest of these pills to your mother," he said. "She can give them to you if you feel bad again."

"How long will they take to work?" Frank asked him.

"In about fifteen minutes you should feel like a new person."

The doctor stepped outside the door, and before he closed it we heard Betty Frances' voice.

"Are you looking for someone?" she asked, "Is something the matter?"

"I'm the ship's doctor," he told her. "One of the boys came and got me. He said that Frank has been seasick."

"Frank!" she gasped. "He just had dinner a short time ago."

"Yes," he said, "and probably that bouillon soup his sister has been getting him has helped him a great deal."

"Bouillon soup too?"

"You couldn't be Mrs. Handy," he said.

"No," she said. "I'm their sitter. Mr. Handy thought Mrs. Handy needed a rest from the children, so they brought me along to take care of them."

"Very commendable," he said. "Here's a bottle of Dramamine pills. They'll help Frank's seasickness. Just give him one a half-hour before each meal."

"Are you sure he needs these?"

"Yes, I am. And I'm surprised that you didn't send for me sooner. He said he's been seasick ever since he came on board."

I heard the doctor's footsteps going away from the stateroom. Harriet was behind me whispering, "Keep Betty Frances out of here!" So I stuck my head out of the door and said, "I feel a lot better already."

Betty Frances sighed. "I find it hard to believe that you have been seasick, Frank Handy. I was under the impression that seasick people can't eat, and you eat like a . . ."

"I forced myself to eat," I said. "I didn't want to die of malnutrition."

She shook her head sadly. "I've got to get back to the little ones in the next stateroom. Are you sure you're all right now?"

"I'm positive," I said.

"Well, if you need any more of these pills, tell me, and I'll give them to you."

I shut the door, and Harriet pulled me down beside

her on the nearest bunk. "Oh, Joe," she said. "I thought Miss Stanhope was going to catch you!"

"So did I for a few minutes," I said. "By the way, thanks for clipping Stanhope. You throw pretty good for a girl."

Harriet actually blushed, and then she said, "We've got to decide what to do. First of all, we've got to find out if Miss Stanhope is a man or not."

"I found out," I said. "He has a scratchy face. He must have to shave three times a day to cover it up."

"Why don't you tell the captain?" Peter asked.

"I think we'd better," Harriet said.

"You know what will happen, don't you? The captain will find out I'm a stowaway, and I'll be in a mess of trouble."

"I guess you're right," Harriet said. "The ship is going to dock at the first Mexican port tomorrow. Maybe you could get off then and phone your father to come and get you."

I leaned over and put my head into my hands. It wasn't that simple. "How about you?" I asked. "The guy who is pretending to be Miss Stanhope will be after you too."

"I forgot about that," Harriet said.

"I didn't."

Harriet giggled and looked pleased with herself. "You're willing to get caught just to save my life. Oh, Joe, you're wonderful!"

"Ugh!" Peter said. "Harriet, you make me sick."

"Shut up, Peter," I told him. Harriet wasn't so bad once you got used to her. "We'll have to work out a plan."

"All right," Harriet said. "Have you got any ideas?"

Frank swung his legs over the bunk and sat up. "That medicine is pretty good," he said. "I'm beginning to feel a lot better already."

Harriet didn't even look up. "Then help us think," she said.

"I've already got a plan," Frank said. There was something funny in his voice that made us all stare at him. His eyes were glittering like the monster's on the Late Weird Show.

"See that porthole?" he said. "First, I'm going to open it. Then I'm going to take the two of you and stuff you through it, and then I'm going to yell, 'Sharks! Sharks! Come see what nice presents old Frank Handy has for you!'"

Harriet and I jumped up, and so did Frank.

"Don't be so horrible, Frank," she said. "We had to save Joe."

"That's right. You had to save him for the sharks," he said.

I tried to look friendly. "I brought the doctor to help you. Remember?"

"You ate my dinner and my breakfast, and my breakfast and my dinner!"

"I didn't really feel right about it," I said.

"And you're wearing my new shirt!"

"I meant to say 'thank you.'"

"Aughhh!" Frank yelled, and leaped at us.

Harriet and I threw the door open and dashed out. I must say that Harriet turned into her horrible self and wasn't any help at all. She just started screaming, "Mama! Mama!" and ran into the next stateroom, locking the door behind her.

At home I practice running the bases a lot, which

really helped me out now that I needed to move fast. I headed down the corridor toward the stairs, with Frank right on my heels. Being half a year older than he was, my legs were just that much longer, and I managed to stay ahead. I took the stairs three at a time up to the promenade deck.

Frank was making an awful clatter behind me. I turned around to see what he was up to.

My heart started banging, and for a minute my legs felt so wobbly that I stumbled. Frank was after me all right, but so was Stanhope!

11

Discovery!

I took a deep breath and made it the rest of the way to the promenade deck. Where to go next? I had no idea. The only thing I could do was find the captain, but I couldn't imagine where he might be. Would he be in his quarters on the boat deck, or on the bridge up on the navigation deck? I had to try them and find out.

I tore down the promenade deck, but it was nearly deserted, and there was no chance of shaking either Frank or Stanhope. I remembered how crowded the café and club were at night, so I made a quick dash through the club door and into the dimly lit room. Dodi was standing right by the door, wearing a fancy long dress and waiting for her turn to perform.

I stopped for just a second. "Help!" I called. "They're after me!"

I don't know whether Dodi did it on purpose or

accidentally, but as she turned around to see who I was talking about, her foot went out to one side, and Stanhope fell right over it, sprawling on the floor, with Frank coming down on top of him.

I stood there, resting a moment, breathing heavily, and up popped Jerry from a nearby table.

"What's going on?" he yelled at Stanhope, who was trying to untangle himself from Frank and get up.

He looked up and pointed at me. "Catch that kid!"

"With pleasure!" Jerry growled and started after me.

"Jerry!" Dodi screamed. "Don't you dare!"

I didn't wait around to see what happened. I beat it out the opposite door, circled back to the stairway, and dashed up to the boat deck. I had noticed the captain's quarters down at the far end. I raced down the corridor and hammered at the door.

No one onswered.

The sound of footsteps came clattering toward me, and I could see what looked like a mob coming after me. I knew what General Custer had felt like. So I ran out the nearest door, past the lifeboats and up the outside stairs.

I poked my head into the door leading to the bridge.

"Hey! Get outa here! No visitors allowed," somebody shouted at me.

"I only want the captain. Is he in here?"

"Naw," someone said. "Why do you want him?"

I didn't have time for explanations. I could hear the footsteps getting closer again. I dashed for the nearest stairs and made it to the top—the sun deck. I ran all the way down to the opposite end and leaned against the wall by the elevator. There was no use running any longer. I was trapped. There wasn't any other place I could go.

The sky was black with just a smattering of stars to light it, and I knew the water would be a lot blacker. It was quiet on the sun deck, and in all the stillness voices carried a long way. I heard Jerry's voice at the opposite end by the stairway. "I'll take this side," he said, "and you take the other. He won't get away from us this time."

"I'm done for," I thought.

Suddenly, with a swishing sound, the elevator doors next to me opened. I stood there and stared at the operator.

"What are you waiting for?" she said, with a mad look on her face. "The way you've been leaning on that button for the last five minutes, I'd think you were in a hurry."

"I am!" I said, jumping into the elevator. "Oh, hurry! Hurry!"

"Where to?"

"Just close the door!" I said. "Hurry!"

I could hear the footsteps getting close.

"Let's go!" I shouted.

"I think someone else is coming for the elevator," she said.

I took a deep breath and crossed my fingers. "Yeah. It's a guy I know," I said. "He's crazy. He's the one who's been telling everyone on the ship that the captain should have hired a *pretty* elevator operator."

"Is that so?" she said, slamming the door.

The elevator began to descend slowly. "All the way down," I told her.

"He'll just have to stay there until I get back up again," she said in an angry voice. "I can't wait around all night."

I thought of where I wanted to go. "Main deck," I said. I was going to the kennels. That old elevator went so slowly I was at the point of wishing my fingernails were long enough to chew on.

As soon as the doors slid back I raced down to the kennels.

The guy in charge turned around and smiled at me. "Where have you been, boy? Your dog has been missing you."

I opened the cage door, and Feef jumped right into my arms, slobbering all over my face with her wet tongue.

"Do me a favor," I asked. "Tell me where I can find the captain. It's an emergency."

"No trouble about that," he said. "All I have to do is pick up this phone on the wall and tell the operator I want the captain. Why do you want to see him?"

"I've got something to tell him about that guy who is missing—that Mr. Riggle."

He hesitated a minute, and I said, "Please trust me. I wouldn't give you the wrong dope."

He picked up the phone and asked somebody to find the captain and send him down to the kennels. I sighed, burying my face in Feef's neck. Now my knees were really wobbling. I thought all I had to do was wait for the captain.

I couldn't have been more wrong. The door opened and there stood Stanhope, glaring at me.

Feef started to growl, and I took a step backward.

I couldn't go any farther. My back was against the cage.

Right after him, Frank and Jerry shoved into the room.

"We watched the elevator light," Frank said. "We saw it go all the way down and knew you'd be here." He frowned. "Now I'm going to give you a poke in the nose."

Poor Feef started to tremble again. I think it was Feef. It couldn't have been me.

"You dumb stowaway, eating all my dinners and breakfasts," Frank yelled.

"Hey, boy," Jerry said, giving Frank a good look, "did you say this kid is a stowaway?"

"That's right," Frank said. "He doesn't even belong on this ship."

Jerry looked at me the way a cat sometimes looks at a cornered mouse, and Stanhope smiled in an ugly way.

"Well," Stanhope said, "that should take care of the problem very nicely."

"What is all this?" the guy in the kennels asked. "What's going on?"

The door pushed open again, and this time the captain came into the room. Jerry and Stanhope and I started to talk at once.

"Just a minute," the captain said. "Ladies first."

Stanhope looked around and then realized he meant her—or him—and said, "This boy is annoying us, Captain."

"I'll say he is!" Jerry added.

116

"And we found out that he's a stowaway," Stanhope said.

The captain stared at me. "Is this true?"

I nodded.

"We've been at sea three days. Where have you been hiding? What have you had to eat?"

Frank spoke up. "My rotten sister Harriet has been hiding him out! I think you should throw her off the ship too!"

I didn't want to get anyone else into trouble. After all, I was used to being in trouble, even though most of the time it wasn't my fault. "Don't blame Harriet," I said. "I came on board in Los Angeles to look around and couldn't get off when everybody left, so I decided to stay on until we got to Mexico and somehow get to my dad. He's working with a movie crew in a town near the Mexican coast."

"This is very serious," the captain said.

The door flew open again, giving Jerry a good whack in the rear, which I didn't mind a bit. Dodi Doll leaped into the room.

"I followed you here," she said. "What are you doing to Joe?"

"He's a stowaway," Jerry told her.

She looked puzzled. "Are you, Joe?"

I only nodded. It was getting hard to talk.

Dodi thought for a long moment. Then she held her shoulders back, lifted her chin, and said, "Captain, Joe is a very nice boy. I'm sure if he's a stowaway, he has a good reason for it."

"He gave us his reason," the captain said.

118

"If I pay his fare will you let him go?"

"Dodi!" Jerry said. "Are you crazy?"

"No," she said. "Joe gave me something. I'm giving him something in return."

I was surprised too. "What did I give you?"

She smiled and reached out to pat my cheek. "You told me I should be happy being a good singer instead of trying so hard to be a terrible actress. Well, I'm taking your advice, and I'm happier already."

"Dodi!" Jerry moaned and covered his face with his hands.

"Don't worry, Jerry," she said. "I'll let you go right on being my agent, and maybe you can work things out so that I can cut a record."

Jerry took his hands down and began to think. Then he actually smiled. "We might have something there!" he said. "I'll get with it immediately!"

Dodi turned to the captain. "Please release Joe. I'll be responsible."

"It's not that simple," the captain said. "Being a stowaway is a serious thing."

He stared down at me, and the way he did it, I felt as though I had shrunk a few inches. "Did you think of how the people at home must feel since your disappearance? How worried they must be about you?"

I really hadn't. I was sure they'd be glad I had gone.

"You can give me their names and your father's location in Mexico, and I'll send word to them that you are safe," the captain said. "Until we dock tomorrow and someone comes to pick you up, you'll be assigned to an empty stateroom and confined to quarters."

"Gee!" Frank said happily. "With a guard?"

"Come along," the captain said.

I had almost forgotten what I was going to say. "Wait a minute!" I said. "I've got something important to tell you."

"I can hear it in my office."

"It has to be right now!"

"Please, Captain," Dodi said. "Let Joe tell you what he wants. It might be important. Every prisoner should be allowed one last request."

"This isn't such a dramatic situation, Miss Doll," the captain said.

"Just let him talk. Please?"

The captain seemed terribly impatient, so I blurted out, "The night before Mr. Riggle disappeared I saw him throw something overboard. It was a package about so big." I tried to use my hands to show him the size I meant and not drop Feef at the same time.

"What's that?" the captain asked.

"You see!" Stanhope looked a lot happier than he had before. "That package must have been the missing bonds from the bank. I told you I had no knowledge of them. Now, when the police come aboard tomorrow to search his cabin, you can tell them that this boy saw them thrown overboard."

"Well, well," the captain said, rubbing his chin. "You're positive of this, boy?"

I shook my head hard. "I'm positive I saw Mr. Riggle

throw something overboard, but it wasn't a package of bonds, whatever they are. It was a package made up of Mr. Riggle's brown suit and shoes."

"What?"

Everybody was looking at me as though I was crazy, and I had to talk fast.

"Remember that nothing is supposed to be missing except the clothes Mr. Riggle wore?"

"That's right. He was wearing them when he disappeared."

"No," I said. "Because Mr. Riggle didn't disappear. Miss Stanhope did."

"I think the kid is going batty," Jerry said.

"Please listen," I told them. "Miss Stanhope is missing because there never was a Miss Stanhope. I was on the gangplank when I heard Mr. Riggle telling the officer that Miss Stanhope was already on board, even though she hadn't been checked off the list of passengers."

I took another deep breath. "Mr. Riggle just pretended there was a Miss Stanhope and paid for two staterooms. Then, the first night out, he threw that brown suit and shoes overboard, shaved off his beard, and became Miss Stanhope."

Everyone turned to Miss Stanhope. "This boy is perfectly ridiculous," she said. "He's the one who has been posing as someone else and making up stories all over the ship. How can we believe anything a stowaway says! Take him away and lock him up!"

Stanhope put out a hand and gave me a push toward the captain, which scared Feef. I guess the

121

poor little dog thought Stanhope was trying to hurt me because she gave a loud growl, leaped out of my arms and at Stanhope.

Stanhope yelled and shook Feef off, but Feef had a good grip on Stanhope's hair, and as she fell, the wig went too. Stanhope stood there looking pretty foolish with part of his disguise gone.

The guy in charge of the kennels had been thinking faster than the rest of us because he had already picked up the ship's phone and called for reinforcements. Maybe Miss Stanhope, or Mr. Riggle, or whatever else anybody wanted to call him, had thought of running, but he didn't have a chance. There were about a dozen men at the door, and after a few words with the captain, they led Mr. Stanhope-Riggle away.

"Oh, Joe," Dodi said, "you make a wonderful detective!"

I thought about all that the captain had said about Mrs. Crumbacher and Cissy worrying about me, and about my father, and what he was going to have to say, and I knew the worst was yet to come.

"No, I'm not," I said. "I'm plain old Joe Riley, and I guess I'm good for nothing except getting into trouble."

12

Good Intentions

The captain took me to a stateroom on the deck where the crew had their cabins. He didn't say much to me, but he had a nice dinner sent up.

I sat there on my bunk, thinking about the guard at my door and missing Feef and wondering if Frank had beat up Harriet yet, and trying to think of something to say to my dad the next morning to keep him from being too mad at me. Before I knew it, I fell asleep.

In the morning a seaman came for me and took me to the bridge to see the captain. The sun was gleaming gold all over everything, and ahead of us lay a town, looking as though it rose right up out of the ocean.

"We're docking there," the captain said. "I thought you might like to watch."

"That's very nice of you, sir," I said. I was glad the captain didn't carry a grudge long.

"Just stay out of the way," he warned me.

I was only too glad to. I found a place for myself near the big glass window and watched the tugs come out to meet the ship and guide it into the harbor and up to the dock. I hadn't thought of how hard it would be to steer such a big thing, and I got so excited watching everything that was going on that it took me a few minutes to recognize a man who was standing way out on the pier.

"There's my father," I said to the captain.

"He informed us he'd be here," the captain said. "In a few minutes I'll turn you over to him."

"Aren't you going to punish me or anything like that?"

The captain's face looked sterner than ever. "I'll leave that to your father."

I gulped. There have been a few times in my life that, after I've done something somebody thought I shouldn't, and Dad has had a session with me, I've found it hard to sit down for awhile. I figured this was going to be one of those times.

But it wasn't exactly. At least not right there on the ship. The captain had Dad escorted to his quarters to meet me, and Dad sat down and told me a lot of the same things the captain had told me, and a few more things about Mrs. Crumbacher worrying and calling the police and finally notifying Dad, and about Dad getting ready to fly home just before he got word I was on the ship.

"You really did it this time, Joe," he said.

"But, Dad," I asked, "aren't you glad to see me? Aren't you going to ask me if I had a nice trip?"

He made sort of a choking noise, so I hurried to tell him the whole story, not leaving anything out, which took a long time.

"So you see," I ended, "nothing was really my fault."

Dad just sighed. Grownups get their minds made up to something and they have an awfully hard time changing them. I decided I wasn't going to be like that when I grew up.

"I think," my dad said, "that this whole episode is going to need a lot more discussing when we get to my hotel."

"I guess so," I said, wondering how long it would be before I'd be able to sit down again.

"First of all, you can write a long letter of apology to Mrs. Crumbacher and another one to Cissy."

"To Cissy too!" I complained.

"I wouldn't argue about it if I were you. You are very much in disgrace."

Somebody had washed my wet clothes, so I sent Frank's dirty ones back to him. Dad ran his comb through my hair, and we got ready to leave the ship.

I was really surprised to see a group of people on deck next to the gangplank. Betty Frances and all the Handy kids were lined up, and they started jumping up and down when they saw me.

Harriet stepped forward and handed me a paper bag. "Inside that bag is a box of chocolates I got for you," she said.

"Gee, thanks, Harriet," I told her.

"Don't worry about some of them being missing," she said. "I ate all the chocolate creams out of it."

"That's O.K."

Harriet looked a little timid for Harriet. "Uh, Joe," she said, "will you write to me?"

The back of my neck got hot, and I said, "I never write to girls."

Harriet looked so miserable, though, that I felt sorry for her. I said, "Well, if you write to me, I might just decide to read the letter, but I won't promise."

She brightened up right away, which just proves how dumb girls can be.

Frank said, "I've got something I'd like to give you, but they won't let me." He stuck his face right into mine. "It's a big punch in the nose!"

"Frank!" Betty Frances said, pulling him back.

Dodi Doll stepped up to say good-bye. She was carrying Feef, and old Feef wiggled and cried trying to get to me. Dodi could hardly hang on to her.

"Better take this silly dog," Dodi said. "She wants to go to you."

I took Feef into my arms and held her closely. She started licking into my ear.

"I'm going to miss you, Feef." I told her. "You were a good friend to me."

"You don't have to miss Feef," Dodi said. "I just gave her to you."

I stared hard at Dodi. I thought maybe Feef had got my ear so wet I couldn't hear right. "You what?"

"I said I gave Feef to you. She's not happy with me, and I don't even want a dog. Besides, she's already proved that she's your dog."

"Oh, gosh!" I said. "Oh, gosh! Oh, thank you!" I stuck my face down in Feef's curly blue hair and hugged her as hard as I could.